Murder at the Races

Book 3

A Dodo Dorchester Mystery by

Ann Sutton

©2020 Ann Sutton

No part of this book may be reproduced in any form whatsoever, whether by graphic, visual, electronic, film, microfilm, tape recording or any other means, without the prior written permission of the author and publisher, except in case of brief critical reviews.

This is a work of fiction. The characters, names, incidents, places and dialogue are products of the author's imagination and are not to be construed as real. The opinions and views expressed herein belong solely to the author.

Permission for the use of sources, graphics and photos is the responsibility of the author.

Published by

>   Wild Poppy Publishing LLC
>   Highland, UT 84003

Distributed by Wild Poppy Publishing

Cover design by Julie Matern
Cover Design ©2020 Wild Poppy Publishing LLC

Edited by Jolene Perry

In Memory of Marjorie Sutton

List of Characters

Lady Dorothea 'Dodo' Dorchester – amateur sleuth and fashion icon
Charlie Chadwick – childhood friend of Dodo
Chief Inspector Blood – Scotland Yard Detective
Violet Guthrie – hostess for Ascot party
Arthur Guthrie – host for Ascot party
Alistair Guthrie – friend of Charlie's
Portia Bodwyn-Jones – guest of Alistair's
Roger Farnsworth – guest of Alistair's
Felicity Snodgrass – guest of Alistair's
Alexander Babcott – boyfriend of Felicity and guest of Alistair
Lord Jeremy Barchester – new Earl and guest of the Guthrie's
Lady Adelaide Barchester – wife of Lord Barchester
Colonel Cuthbert Winchester – member of Prime Minister's cabinet and friend of the Guthries
Margaret Winchester – wife of the colonel
Lady Guinevere Dorchester – Dodo's mother
Lancelot Betram – cousin of Lord Barchester
Sally – a barmaid

Table of Contents

Chapter 1 1
Chapter 2 10
Chapter 3 16
Chapter 4 26
Chapter 5 37
Chapter 6 45
Chapter 7 53
Chapter 8 62
Chapter 9 71
Chapter 10 79
Chapter 11 88
Chapter 12 97
Chapter 13 105
Chapter 14 111
Chapter 15 118
Chapter 16 126
Chapter 17 134
Chapter 18 144
Chapter 19 156
Chapter 20 164
Chapter 21 174
About the Author 179

Chapter 1

Ascot 1923

A frisson of excitement tickled Lady Dorothea's insides as the military brass band belted out patriotic tunes and the red, white, and blue flags snapped in the steady, summer breeze. The marriage of the royal presence, the throbbing music and the air of celebration, culminated in a glorious euphoria that brought back memories of the Kings' coronation and made this an occasion to remember.

She checked her dress and hat as she approached the Royal Couple. The Honorable Lady Dorothea Dorchester dropped into a low, respectful curtsey. His Royal Highness, King George V, cut a dashing figure in full military uniform and Her Royal Highness, Queen Mary, beautifully outshone her husband in a splendid formal gown, a royal sash across the shoulder.

It was a misconception that if you were a member of the English aristocracy you rubbed shoulders with the monarchy all the time. Dorothea, or Dodo to her friends, had been presented to the King when she'd come out, along with all the other debutantes, of course, and had attended a couple of Royal Garden Parties with her parents, but her family were certainly not considered part of the inner circle of intimate friends of the King and Queen.

Even though Dodo considered herself a modern woman and a forward thinker, she clung to the pomp and ceremony of the monarchy as much as anyone else. It set Great Britain apart from most of the other countries of the world. So, when Charlie Chadwick had invited her to Royal Race Day at Ascot with the understanding that he had managed to secure a separate invitation for a personal attendance with the King and Queen of England, she could not turn it down.

Now, as Dodo dipped, head bowed, allowing the clipped accents of the King and Queen to wash over her, she experienced a burst of love for her country. Dodo knew that there was a rising rebellion against the whole institution of monarchy in the modern era but something about it still fascinated and enthralled her. She was a part of all this, and the knowledge filled her with pride.

Almost as soon as the introduction began, it was over and she was ushered to the side to exit the royal area, passing several military attendants who provided security for the King and Queen.

"That was a bit of fun, eh?" Charlie's ocean-blue eyes twinkled. Dodo was sure her face betrayed her infatuation with the encounter as her eyes brimmed with patriotic tears.

"Rather," she said with enthusiasm. "How on earth did you manage to get a pass?"

"My father did something to get the King's attention this year and was given the passes as a reward. Makes the whole occasion more memorable."

Charlie was an old and dear friend, but from the look currently dancing in his friendly eyes, she suspected he was hoping for more.

Was she?

They had met up again recently at a country party that had ended disastrously. A maid had been murdered. In fact, Dodo had helped find the murderer. But more to the point, she had received this royal invitation after a failed romance in Paris. Charlie's timing was perfect. With a slightly bruised heart, she had welcomed the chance to attend the Royal Meeting at Ascot, coupled with a visit to Charlie's parent's home for the week.

Just them. No party. No pressure. No expectations. Or so she thought.

Am I ready for another relationship? Perhaps.

Dodo shielded her eyes from the July sun. "Meeting their Royal Highnesses was simply marvelous! And now I'm famished!"

He grinned through his tousled brown hair, eyes crinkling. "Let's go and find our box, then."

Charlie, whose greatest strength was his ability to make and keep friends, had managed to inveigle an invitation to the private venue. She allowed him to take her by the hand, though she didn't yet consider them a couple, and find the stairs that led to the private viewing box.

Dodo looked around her enthusiastically as they mounted the steps. The whole racecourse was decked out like a vain duchess, bunting and flags everywhere, beckoning participants to indulge in their vices.

Dodo may not have been fond of the racing itself particularly, but the atmosphere was undeniably intoxicating; the pull of the chance to meet the King and Queen, dress up in one's finest and socialize with the highest society England had to offer, indisputable.

The stands were already quite full as they ascended, and Dodo experienced a familiar thrill as she looked out over the many hats and dresses that had been especially tailored for the day's events. Fashion was the thing that really made her blood sing. As an ambassador for the French fashion House of Dubois and a couple of British ones, Dodo had an experienced eye, and a lot of opinions on clothing. Her own clothes always made a statement. Royal Race Day was no exception. She had worked with British fashion designer Norman Hartnell to produce something different that would inspire her and make waves in the society press.

The result was a flowing dress in blush peach that sported an uneven hem, edged in a broad but delicate lace. The whole thing was cinched with a thick fabric band that sat atop her hips and was secured with a large bow in the front. The top of the dress was quite plain with a straight line and thin straps, but a sheer, overlay flutter cape, edged with the same lace as the hem, was thrown over the top. The overlay hung down to the belt bow at the front and back in a dramatic triangle. It was quite unlike anything else she had seen. A cloche hat covered in the same fabric and lace and adorned with a tasteful flower bow, and peach satin shoes completed the look. The whole outfit gave her an edge, a confidence that only money could buy. Not that she needed the boost, but it was nice anyway.

Charlie, who normally dressed with an air of negligent stylishness, was deliciously decked out in the traditional morning suit required by Ascot, charcoal gray tails paired with gray, pinstripe trousers, an ash gray waistcoat and snow-white shirt with an ascot tie. Dodo had a weakness for full morning suits.

As they left the royal enclosure, he gently held her hand like a proposition for more than friendship, as they climbed the stairs, his touch triggering a happy warmth.

At the top they showed their passes. Dodo looked into the intimate space with tables groaning under the weight of exotic foods. She was impressed that their hosts had spared no expense. King prawns proudly grabbed the edge of silver stands filled with caviar. Stuffed beef Wellington and pheasant adorned other platters. Fluffy pastries bulging with cream overflowed from crystal cake stands. Even her grandmother, the Dowager, would approve.

Dodo's tummy grumbled with pleasure and anticipation now that the excitement of meeting the King and Queen had passed.

Once permitted to enter, she glanced around the room, seeing a pair of older couples and a table full of young people engaged in boisterous conversation. A young man, a good head taller than everyone else, was striding toward them, whom she supposed to be Charlie's friend. He was lanky with a friendly smile and a shock of red hair.

"Charlie!" the red-headed fellow said, grabbing him by the hand and shaking it with real affection. "So glad you could make it."

He turned to Dodo. "And this vision of loveliness needs no introduction. You are very welcome, Lady Dorothea." With gracious chivalry he took her outstretched hand and placed a formal kiss on it.

"You flatter me..." She hesitated not knowing his name.

"Oh heavens! How ill-mannered of me," said Charlie. "Dodo, this is my good friend Alistair Guthrie. We're up at Cambridge together."

"Thank you, Alistair." Dodo flashed her best smile and witnessed the poor chap melt before her eyes. He cleared his throat. "Let me introduce you around. Do you know anyone, Charlie?"

Charlie scanned the room. "No," he said simply.

Alistair beckoned them and Charlie took Dodo's hand again as they followed him to the group at the table.

"Everyone, this is an old pal of mine, Charlie Chadwick and the lovely Lady Dorothea Dorchester."

"Oh goodness!" she exclaimed. "Just call me Dodo."

A pretty blonde looked up at her with narrowed eyes, covering an angry scar on her cheek with her hand, and a mousy-haired girl in a polka dot horror was all smiles. An intense dark fellow seated next to the blonde, scowled and an angular man grinned at her like a puppy dog.

"Alexander Babbcott, his girlfriend Felicity Snodgrass," said Alistair indicating the blonde with his hand. "Portia Bodwyn-Jones and Roger Farnsworth."

"Lovely to meet you," said the polka-dotted Portia.

The blonde continued to regard Dodo with suspicion, a reaction Dodo was accustomed to with other good-looking females. She determined to try to win her over.

"It's a pleasure," replied Dodo in her most ingratiating manner.

"Come and grab some food," said Alistair, "and then you can join everyone."

They followed him to where one of the older couples were filling their plates.

"Those are friends of my parents, who should be here at any moment. Colonel and Mrs. Winchester." Alistair dropped his voice. "The colonel may look familiar. He is part of the Prime Minister's cabinet."

Dodo sneaked a sideways glance. There *was* something familiar about him, though she had no particular interest in politics.

"And over by the window," Alistair continued, "the newly minted Lord Barchester. His uncle died without issue and the title came to him. And that's his wife, Lady Barchester. When my parents get here that will round us out."

The new Lady Barchester had the swollen middle of many older women. Her seamstress had made a valiant effort to disguise it with a drop-waist gown, but it hugged her in all the wrong places.

Dodo gave her points for trying.

Famished, Dodo loaded her plate with juicy king prawns, cocktail sauce and some caviar, then picking up a flute of champagne, followed Charlie back to the table where a fiery debate was raging between the two young men. Dodo thought the girls looked bored and didn't blame them.

Politics. What bad manners. Hadn't they been taught that religion and politics were taboo in polite conversation?

Charlie, ever the knight in shining armor, did not enter the debate, instead rescuing Felicity from her boredom. One of the things Dodo had always appreciated about Charlie was his knack for making friends. Even as a teenager, he could quickly put strangers at ease and always gave them his undivided attention. So few people really did that. Dodo watched as Charlie worked this same magic on the dour Felicity whose hard exterior began to soften, though she kept her hand up to hide the ugly blemish on her cheek. It really was a nasty disfigurement that looked pretty fresh. Dodo's inquisitive mind sprang to life.

I'd love to know how Felicity got that scar. Not the sort of question one asks a stranger.

"And how do you know Alistair?" Charlie asked Felicity, his ruggedly handsome face open and sincere.

"We met last year on a holiday in the West Indies. He tried teaching us to sail. It was marvelous." Her upper-class voice came with a slightly nasal tone. "Alistair invited me today and said I could bring someone." She glanced at the intense young man beside her. "This is Alex." The debater did not stop his fevered speech and Felicity did not smile as she said his name. Dodo idly wondered why they were even together.

Felicity turned back to Charlie. "How about you?" Felicity did not include Dodo in the question.

"Alistair and I are in the same year at Cambridge and shared a tutor last year."

Alexander suddenly hit the table with his palm.

Dodo started.

"These two are discussing the rise of fascism in Germany," explained Portia, pulling her lips down.

"Really? How perfectly awful!" declared Dodo. "Shouldn't today be a little more light-hearted than that?"

The angst-filled, darker Alexander opened his black eyes wide with shock, while Roger laughed and slapped him on the back. "She's right, old man. It's a holiday. We're boring the ladies."

Alexander suddenly looked like a frustrated dissenter that pitied the people around him for not having the intelligence to see things from his point of view.

"Boring the ladies?" he repeated in disbelief.

"Yes, you are," muttered Felicity.

"*We* just had an audience with the King," Charlie announced to lighten the mood.

"Did you, now?" said Alistair, impressed by this piece of information.

"Archaic institution if you ask me," said Alexander. "Can't see it lasting much longer."

Felicity slapped his arm. "What a shockingly awful thing to say," she gasped. "Not everything is a debate, Alex."

Alexander picked up his glass and drank rather than commenting.

"Darlings!" an impossibly high voice screeched from across the room. A reed thin woman with the hereditary red hair was bounding towards them wearing a frightful mismatch of colors and an enormous hat with enough feathers to clothe a tropical bird.

"Here's Mother," muttered Alistair, standing to welcome her. A short, fat fellow followed in her wake.

Alistair made the introductions again while his mother squealed with delight at each name. Dodo could feel a headache coming on and looked daggers at Charlie, who by the look of his tight, red cheeks was trying hard not to laugh.

"Welcome to our little party," Mrs. Guthrie gushed. "I do so love to spend time with the young. It is so enlivening."

"Darling," said her husband. "We are late and should welcome our other guests." Mrs. Guthrie's face fell for an instant and then resumed its over-bright smile as she followed her husband over to Lord and Lady Barchester.

"Apologies," whispered Alistair, his skin matching his hair. "Mother has recently discovered cocktails and has taken rather a liking to them."

Everyone mumbled that they hadn't noticed, and the conversation was steered in other directions.

Dodo was still hungry and excused herself to go back to the food table while Charlie chatted with Alistair.

As she approached, Mrs. Winchester was wiping her husband's collar with a napkin, her eyes intense and thin, her voice urgent. "Don't worry."

But the lines on his face betrayed his concern.

Dodo supposed that ministers in government had many worries pressing on them all the time and attached little importance to the interaction.

Though Alex had tamed his rhetoric when she returned to the table, Dodo was relieved when the announcer called the King's Stakes race and Charlie suggested they go out onto the deck to get a good view.

Everyone followed suit.

"We didn't place a bet," Dodo pointed out.

"No," Charlie replied, stringing out the word. "Remember? I'm a reformed man."

Idiot! How insensitive. How could I have forgotten?

"Of course. How silly of me." Heat flashed on her cheek at her faux pas. "Let's just look at the jockey's colors and choose the one we want to win."

Charlie placed his hand over hers on the railing. "Splendid. Do you have any horses in this race?"

"No. My father isn't coming until tomorrow with *Caspian* and *Arabian*. I've supported the family business several times this year, so Daddy was happy to let me come to the royal race today."

Charlie produced a pair of binoculars and handed them to Dodo. Looking through the lenses she saw the jockeys pulling on the reins to keep their steeds still, a row of bright colors, steady but in constant motion.

"Purple. I'm going to choose the purple jockey." She handed the binoculars back.

"Black and white." Charlie dropped the lenses and his gaze collided with hers. He gave her a slow, devastating smile that transformed his features from pleasant to seriously attractive. He was definitely sending a message about his intentions, but though she found him handsome, she felt no reciprocal spark in her blood. Yet.

But I am happy to be converted.
The loudspeaker crackled into action.
"And they're off!"

Chapter 2

Everyone in the stands below was shouting and whistling. Dodo allowed herself to be caught up in the fervor, waving her hands and smacking the balustrade. She was surprised how fun it was to cheer on your horse – especially when you had nothing to lose.

As it happened, Charlie's horse won.

"What a shame I didn't have that kind of luck when it mattered," he joked in a self-deprecating manner.

Dodo touched his arm. "It takes a strong man to admit when he has a problem. I'm impressed that you had the backbone to stop."

Charlie glanced at her, sincerity stamped on his forehead. "Really?"

"Yes. We've both seen what backbreaking debt can lead to." She turned to face him.

Charlie nodded. "Murder you mean?"

"Yes," Dodo replied. "My visit to France wasn't much different. Crushing debt led to a murder there too."

Charlie's brows shot up. "Murder? It seems to follow you, m'lady."

"That's what my maid Lizzie says." She turned back to the track, a grim smile on her lips. "But I seem to have a talent for ferreting out the culprits."

"You helped the police again?" Charlie asked, moving closer to Dodo, his arms resting on the railing, barely touching hers.

"I didn't work *with* them so much as in parallel. The French inspector was rather offended by my presence."

Charlie threw back his head and laughed. "I can well imagine!" He turned to her. "What was the name of that chap from Scotland Yard that came to solve the case of the maid? Blatt…Blott…"

"Blood."

"Oh yes, Inspector Blood. I should have remembered since it was something Dickensian. *He* seemed to welcome your help."

"It's Chief Inspector Blood, actually," she replied. "And only after I tamed him."

The loudspeaker crackled again as another race was set to begin.

"I'm rather thirsty, shall we go back in?" Charlie asked.

The staff had placed a silver urn of tea on the food table. It was a welcome addition. Most of the party had followed them out on to the deck but Lord Barchester and his wife quickly drew apart as they entered the box. From the color on the new peer's cheek, it was clear they had been having a disagreement.

Lady Barchester moved over to join Dodo at the tea table. "I simply love your dress!" The compliment was half-hearted, as though she had made herself say it.

"Thank you. I had it specially designed by Norman Hartnell." Dodo checked Lady Barchester's face to see if the name meant anything. Apparently not.

"I shall have to pay him a visit." She looked down at her own frock and smoothed it over her ample waist. "I understand your parents are Alfred and Guinevere Dorchester. I met them several months ago at a dinner party when we were first introduced into society. I was terrified but your mother was so kind. I simply love her. So full of such joie de vivre."

This was an apt description of Dodo's vivacious and handsome mother and she agreed.

"I am rather new to all this"—Lady Barchester waved her hand at the box—"and your mother was very accepting. It is not an easy thing to break into."

"I'm sure you are right," said Dodo. "People can be quite suspicious of new inductees and terrible snobs."

"Quite, quite." Lady Barchester's eyes darted left and right as though she worried that to agree would be offensive. She took a sip of her tea. "It has taken some adjustment for Jeremy too. Had to give up his job in the City. He is so used to being engaged." She placed the cup down on the table and swept a hand across her brow. "He was in the army before we met, you know. He's a man of many talents." Her eyes found her husband who was talking to

Mr. Guthrie. They held a hint of fear. Perhaps she was afraid that she did not measure up to his new position in society.

The door to the balcony opened again and Alistair's mother walked in. Dodo felt an involuntary desire to flee but Mrs. Guthrie hastened towards her and grabbed her hand. "I am so happy to have a celebrity in our midst," she gushed, revealing her prominent teeth. "I follow your work with the House of Dubois and here too. I am fascinated with fashion myself."

You could have fooled me.

Dodo checked the uncharitable thought. "I am very fortunate. It is an exciting profession."

"Have you and Charlie been seeing each other long?" Mrs. Guthrie dipped her head as though she expected Dodo to reveal her innermost desires, but the expression reminded Dodo of her pony, Bluebell, expecting a treat and she raised her hand to hide a smile.

"Actually, we are just old friends and he thought I might like to come since he had the special invitation to meet the King and Queen. Our parents have been friends for decades."

"Me thinks the lady doth protest too much," said Mrs. Guthrie with a vulgar wink.

Dodo could feel embarrassment blossom inside, ready to bloom across her face. "Oh, no it's not like that. Really."

"Someone had better tell Charlie," chuckled Mrs. Guthrie. "He's such a lovely boy."

Dodo followed her gaze to where Charlie was standing by the window, watching her. Seeing him through someone else's eyes, she experienced a kind of epiphany. He actually looked rather seductive in his formal suit and summer tan, blue eyes blazing. She had once described him as nice. N.I.C.E. And he was. But could he be more? Did she want him to be more? His high cheekbones perfectly set the stage for his full mouth and square chin. The sad fact was that, as good-looking as he undoubtably was, he still failed to ignite a glow in her. Perhaps it was their childhood history that muddied the waters. Seeing him now, she wished she could conjure up some chemistry.

The next race ended, and the rest of the party came into the box from the balcony, breaking their connection.

As the young people settled back at the table with plates loaded with food, Colonel Winchester pulled out a chair to join them. Alexander bristled.

"It is so good to mingle with the young," the colonel began in a raspy voice that hinted at years of smoking. "You are the leaders of tomorrow after all." His skin was mottled and great mutton-chop white, whiskers clung to his flabby jaw. "How are you enjoying the day?"

"It's simply marvelous," gushed Portia, popping a cream cake into her mouth. "Nothing like a day at Ascot."

"And the good weather helps," added Roger. "One year it rained the entire day. Quite put a damper on things."

"Dorothea and I had the privilege of meeting the King and Queen...though I am sure the King is no stranger to you." Charlie turned his palms over expressively as he directed the question at the colonel.

Colonel Winchester puffed out his chest. "I do not associate with him as often as you might imagine," he replied, stroking his white whiskers. His thinning hair was heavily doctored with oil but was failing in its duty to hide his bald head. "Of course, the Prime Minister has regular meetings with His Royal Highness."

Alexander's face flinched as though he had bitten into a bad piece of fish.

"What's he like? The Prime Minister?" asked Felicity.

"Splendid chap. Trustworthy to a fault. A man of his word." The colonel sounded like a political radio advertisement.

Dodo didn't trust him.

Her uncle had a prize bull that was a nasty piece of work. She realized that Alexander was looking at the politician with the same expression her uncle reserved for the bull. Felicity's face was furrowed with worry.

The colonel continued. "Just the other day the Prime Minister said, 'Winchester, I told the widows and orphan's fund director that I would host a fundraiser for his charity. Let's set about it.' I reminded him that my area of expertise is the armed forces and that I might not be the right man for that particular job when, without missing a beat, he said, 'Have you met his wife? You might need to bring all your skills to bear working with her!'"

Colonel Winchester's shoulders shot up and the most unique sound emanated from his mouth—a cross between a sheep and a hyena.

Everyone around the table, with the exception of Alexander who was still pretending to be outraged, was trying to hide their shock.

"Cuthbert," warned the colonel's wife from across the room, "I am sure the young people do not share your unique sense of humor." She wore a tight, embarrassed smile on her pudgy face and the feathers on her singular, pink hat were trembling. "Let's leave them to socialize on their own, shall we?"

The colonel looked around the table to gauge the truth of her remark. His expression fell faster than a dead pheasant. "Duty calls," he said, his change of heart telling Dodo that he was upset that his dowdy wife was spoiling his fun. "Toodle loo!"

He pushed back his chair and walked over to Mrs. Winchester who was talking with Alistair's parents.

"What an awful chap!" croaked Alexander. "Establishment booby."

"Oh, for goodness sake!" cried Felicity. "Can't you leave the revolutionary clap-trap out of it. You're spoiling a lovely day." She stalked off to the drinks table.

Alexander sunk into a quiet, brooding moodiness which was a much better condition in Dodo's opinion.

"Did anyone win anything on that last race?" *Good old Charlie.* His comment broke the tension and smoothed over the awkwardness the interchange had caused.

Dodo glanced over to see Lord Barchester approach the colonel. The minister looked into his eyes with intensity as Lord Barchester asked a question and then shook his head, followed by a guffaw of laughter. Then he slapped the new peer on the shoulder and went to join his wife.

Thank heavens he didn't repeat that awful animal sound!

Several of the people at the table had lost money on the last race and were sharing stories of other large successes. Alexander was still sitting, arms crossed, shoulders hunched in stony silence looking like a petulant schoolboy. Felicity had returned and was edging her chair closer and closer to Charlie.

I don't think her relationship with Alexander will last much longer.

With Alexander finally on mute, Portia shared some funny stories about her family. She may have no fashion sense, but she had a marvelous personality.

A little before four o' clock, Charlie suggested they both go back out on the deck to watch a race. Dodo eagerly accepted, ready to be back out in the fresh air. She knocked shoulders with someone on the way through the door and had to straighten her hat. Pulling open her clutch bag, she found a little mirror to check her reflection.

"What a bore that Alexander is," Charlie said as they leaned their arms on the handrail. "I know too many chaps like him at Cambridge. All anger and revolution. I give them a wide berth."

Charlie's hand landed gently on hers again as she held onto the railing. It felt…good.

"Yes, he is rather a killjoy."

All at once, the announcer went quiet and the band stopped playing, leaving the muted murmur of the crowd as the only background.

Charlie shifted. "I was thinking… maybe we could—"

His sentence was cut short as a blood-chilling scream rent the quiet air like a massive sail being ripped from its mast in a storm.

Chapter 3

An eerie silence draped over the horrified crowd like a shroud over a corpse, as the hysterical screaming continued to echo around the stadium. Dodo's singular warning system activated.

Even as the spectators remained paralyzed, the race officials began to move. Dodo's eyes locked onto the men in racecourse uniforms as they wove through the people, trickling down the rows and stairs like black ants searching for a grain of sugar.

"Come on!" Dodo grabbed Charlie's arm.

He frowned.

"Let's go and see what's happened." Dodo's curiosity was bursting.

Charlie followed as she tripped down the stairs. Her pulse was drumming in her ears, a mixture of morbid curiosity and flaming fear.

Ensuring that Charlie was still behind her, she threaded her way through the crowds of pretentious hats and followed the officials who were still dribbling in.

Dodo pulled up sharp. Under the stands, Lady Barchester was crouched, oblivious of her gown, hands to her face, head down, her screams spent. Beside her on the floor, lay the crumpled form of a man.

The first official on the scene stood from a kneeling position, palm up to arrest the approach of anyone else. Dodo obeyed and Charlie bumped into her, eyes wide in horror as he spotted the body.

"Good heavens!" he exclaimed. "Is that…?"

"Someone alert the police," cried the official.

Dodo stood rooted to the spot, her natural inclination for sleuthing fighting with her social conscience that argued that she should retreat and let the police handle everything.

"We should go," whispered Charlie in her ear.

"Wait…"

Lady Barchester looked up and caught Dodo's eye. She stood, bent with shock, and beckoned her over.

"Come on," Dodo insisted quietly.

They moved forward slowly, pushing through the small crowd of officials that had gathered around the body. Dodo started the moment she recognized the body as Lord Barchester.

Not shock then. Grief.

Tears were tracking down Lady Barchester's lined face, her hat sitting at a dangerous angle, hem soiled.

She reached out a desperate hand to Dodo while the other was balled into a fist, pressed against her mouth.

Dodo cut her eyes over to the corpse. The back was facing her, but she could see the knife cuts in the jacket clearly, and blood oozing, forming a dark pool around him. Three large lacerations suggested that the murder had been committed in a fit of anger.

Without warning, Lady Barchester drooped into Dodo's arms. Desperate to survey the scene before it was all trampled, she gently pushed Lady Barchester into Charlie's arms. His eyes flared in panic.

"Just keep a hold of her until she comes round, said Dodo, patting his arm."

He nodded, brow furrowing.

Creeping closer to the body, Dodo walked around it with slow, short steps examining the ground. It was mostly dirt since the sun's rays never stretched under here, with the exception of a few weeds. The ground itself was quite dry and hard but not dusty. Evidence of footsteps were everywhere but there was no way to tell if they were recent or months old.

She moved to face the body of the man she had only recently met. His eyes were staring straight ahead which might mean that he was caught by surprise. She looked away.

"Let's form a circle around the body until the police come," said a man with a clipboard.

She would have to move fast.

Avoiding his face, she glanced over Lord Barchester's clothing and decided to look in his pockets before the body was moved. She needed a diversion since the race officials were gathering and she didn't want to be caught.

"How is Lady Barchester? Is she still unwell?" Dodo called out, waving her arm towards Charlie who was still holding the fainting woman, ensuring that her voice was louder than entirely necessary. All heads turned to look at them and Dodo used the moment to crouch down and slip her lithe fingers into the inside pockets of his lordship's morning coat. In the second pocket she felt a folded piece of paper that she pulled out.

Bingo.

It was a betting stub and scrawled on it were the words, *I must meet you. Four o' clock under the east stand.*

Dodo jumped back up and flicked her gaze to the uninspiring middle-aged man at her feet. *A lover?*

She tucked the paper into her dress to give to the police when they arrived.

"Oy! Excuse me miss," said a race official, "but I must ask you to move away."

"Of course," she replied thankful that she had found what she needed.

Stepping back to Charlie and Lady Barchester, she locked eyes with Charlie and then put her arms around the revived but traumatized widow.

"Alright, alright." An officious voice floated through the crowd, eventually revealing a young bobby who must have been assigned to the races today. "What have we here?"

"Excuse me, constable," Dodo began, pushing herself forward. "This is the victim's wife. She is the one who found him."

"Victim?"

Dodo moved aside to reveal the body. The constable blanched.

The young policeman was no more than twenty-three, a slight, pimply youth, unlikely mature enough for regular shaving. His eyes darted from the body, to the widow, to Dodo and then the crowd, his initial officious bluster effectively doused. Taking a deep breath, he pulled out a black leather notebook with a slight shudder, his fingers trembling as he turned the pages.

He plucked the strap of his helmet and then searched his pockets for a pencil.

"Perhaps you should have a look at the body first?" Dodo suggested.

The policeman's brow rose, and he narrowed his eyes in the direction of the corpse. His pallor betrayed his inexperience. "Ah, yes. Of course. If you will excuse me a moment."

The race officials had now successfully formed a protective ring around the body, and they parted to let the policeman through. Dodo watched with interest as his eyes met the victim's empty stare. Abruptly, the young officer turned and ran some yards away before losing the contents of his stomach.

Dodo grimaced.

First timer.

She thought back to the first time *she* had seen a dead body. It certainly had a gut-wrenching physical effect.

The officer bent over, wiping his mouth with the back of his hand, catching his breath.

Lady Barchester's skin was damp and pale, and Dodo thought she might faint again. She glanced at her watch. Four-thirty. "Would you take Lady Barchester up to the box?" Dodo asked Charlie. "I'll let them know where she is." She forced a weak smile as Charlie nodded, gently guiding the weeping woman back to the stairs.

Appreciating the inexperience of the officer, Dodo made the decision to hold onto the damning note until someone more hardened appeared.

The constable stumbled back. "Tell the announcer to stop the races and ask everyone to stay where they are," he said to an official. Dodo was impressed with his presence of mind given that his stomach had just turned inside out.

The policeman walked around to the back of the body and took note of the stab wounds. Then he began tiptoeing around, searching the ground. Dodo watched.

The officer looked up. "Who found the body?"

"The wife," said an official. "I heard screaming and when I arrived, she was crouched by the body."

"And where is she now?"

"I sent her back to the box to get a cup of tea. I hope that's alright? She's in shock," said Dodo.

"And who are you?" he asked.

"I am one of the party in the private box where she is a guest."

He looked back at the official. "Was there anyone else around when you first found her?"

"No. sir."

"What about a weapon?"

"No weapon."

"All right. Let's keep this guard around the body until my superiors get here." He raised his voice. "Everyone else, please go back to where you were when the body was discovered."

The inclination to stay and watch the professionals when they arrived was strong, but Dodo prudently obeyed his request and went back to the box.

As she entered, she saw that the older people were all crowded around Lady Barchester while the younger people were sitting on the far side of the room darting nervous glances at the widow.

Dodo joined the young people.

"Stabbed?" asked Roger in a hoarse whisper, fingering his boutonniere.

"Yes," replied Dodo. "Three times. Someone was very angry with him."

"I hadn't even met him before today," said Portia, running her hands over the skirt of her polka-dot dress. "Poor man."

"Me neither," said Roger.

"You'd met him before, hadn't you Felicity?" said Alexander.

An unidentifiable emotion flashed beneath the surface of Felicity's defensive expression, contrasting with the red scar. "What? No. I mean, yes. Not really, though. He was at some dinner party I attended some months ago." Her hand flew to cover the blemish.

Hmmm.

"When will we be able to leave, do you think?" asked Alexander.

"Not yet," she replied. "Right now, there is only a local bobby at the scene. No one will be able to go until someone higher up arrives." Charlie reached for her hand and she sat down.

"Do you think anyone will mind if we eat?" Portia was eyeing the plates of delicacies beckoning from the tables.

A stress eater.

Everyone else looked at her sideways but mumbled that they supposed it would be alright.

"Who was this 'Lord Barchester'?" asked Charlie to the table at large.

"I don't know him very well myself," admitted Alistair. "A great uncle died or something and suddenly he became lord of the manor."

"Funny how these things turn out," said Charlie.

"Yes. I think he did something in the City before that. Not sure what." Alistair ran a hand over his flaming hair as he watched Lady Barchester's distress.

"And Lady Barchester?" prodded Dodo.

"I believe she is the daughter of a banker. Small town stuff. Not at all used to all this." He swung his arm indicating the box and the racecourse. "Bit out of her league if you ask me. Mother was trying to mentor her."

Dodo looked at Lady Barchester whose eyes were glazed over as though unaware of her surroundings. She was being comforted by Alistair's mother and Mrs. Winchester.

What will happen to her now?

"Do they have any children?" Dodo asked.

"No. It's just the two of them, I understand." Alistair looked over at the huddle of women. He frowned. "I suppose she will be deposed by the next lucky winner of the title."

"Such an archaic system," complained Alexander who had been silent until now.

"Oh, be quiet!" cried Felicity. "Your mother is from a titled family and you have done very well out of it."

A splash of scarlet lit up Alexander's cheek.

Just a pretender then.

Alistair's father and Colonel Winchester were crowded together, whispering in the corner. The atmosphere in the room was tense and outside only the chatter of the crowd was left since all the races had been stopped.

Fortunately, the King and Queen had left after the Royal Race, otherwise that would have added another layer of difficulty to the situation for the police force.

In Dodo's experience, it was advantageous to get people's recollections as soon after a crime as possible. Memories were fickle. Perhaps she could discover something useful to tell the detectives when they arrived.

"Were you in the room or on the deck when the screaming started?" Dodo asked the group, trying to remember herself who else had been out there with them.

"Felicity went out to use the ladies' but the rest of us were in here, I think. We were all in constant motion between the food and the decking, so it's hard to remember," Portia replied, narrowing her eyes in concentration.

"Yes, I did visit the ladies'," admitted Felicity. "I heard the screaming when I was coming back up the stairs."

"What about the older people?" continued Dodo. "Obviously, Lord Barchester was not here, but did anyone notice his wife leave?"

Alistair raised a finger. "I saw Lord Barchester leave. He said he was going out but would be back shortly. I heard him tell his wife. She must have got tired of waiting and gone to find him."

"What time would that have been?"

"It was well after the Royal Race. We all went out on the balcony for that, remember. I think he left before the race at three forty-five."

Dodo glanced at her watch. It was now five. She calculated that the body had been discovered about forty minutes before. So, the murder had occurred between three forty-five and four twenty. A pretty narrow window.

"And the others?"

Alistair spoke again. "Mother was having a fine old chat with the minister. I do remember that because he looked like he would rather be anywhere else."

"And were your father and the colonel's wife involved in the conversation?"

"I say! What are you suggesting?" Alistair's heckles were rising.

"No offense, old thing!" Charlie jumped in. "Dodo has quite the reputation as a sleuth. She's just doing her thing."

Thank you, Charlie.

Alistair fixed his tie and pulled down his coat. "Oh. A gumshoe, eh?"

"I prefer, lady detective," she said, adjusting her hat. "So sorry if I offended you, I just know people forget things and it's good to establish where everyone was."

Alistair looked off into the distance. "I remember Father and Mrs. Winchester were enjoying the caviar but I have no idea what time that was… I actually popped out right at four."

Dodo tipped her head.

Alistair's face exploded in a blush. "I went to meet someone. A friend. Sally."

Dodo couldn't help raising her eyebrows.

That would need explaining later.

"I was here the whole time," grunted Alexander, puffing air through his unruly, dark locks. "Didn't see what anyone else was doing, though."

"Me too," added Roger. "I didn't pay attention to the older people. Sorry."

Dodo knew that she and Charlie had been out on the balcony watching the race, which meant that she had no idea who was where at all.

Dodo wandered over to Lady Barchester whose color was better as she sipped some tea.

"I am so sorry," Dodo began. "Is there anything I can do?"

Lady Barchester lifted her tear-stained face. She wore a look of utter confusion. "Who would do this?" she whimpered. It was just the opening Dodo had been looking for.

"Was your husband meeting someone?"

"No. Why do you ask? He said he was just popping down to collect his winnings and would be back before I knew he was gone. After half an hour I went in search of him."

So, he had lied to his wife about a meeting. Now we are getting somewhere.

"Why did you go under the stands, if I may ask?"

Lady Barchester placed the cup back in the unsteady saucer before answering. "I had walked along everywhere looking for him and a bird under the stand caught my eye. As I watched it hop around, I noticed what I thought was a coat someone had dropped. It wasn't till I got close that I …" She broke down in another bout of tears.

Dodo remained quiet and reached for Lady Barchester's hand giving it a squeeze. After several minutes, she wiped her eyes with a handkerchief, and blew her nose.

"Was there anyone who had anything against your husband?" asked Dodo.

"There was another cousin, Lancelot Bertram, who thought he was next in line—that's why it was such a shock that it was us. But he seemed to get over it."

Did he though? Titles are highly coveted.

Dodo committed the name to memory. "How about today? Did he see anyone he recognized?"

"Not that he told me," she replied, dabbing at her mouth. "We're pretty new to this scene. Just trying to find our footing…I suppose it won't matter anymore. It will all go to the cousin now. I'm just plain Mrs. Barchester again."

"Lady Barchester?"

Dodo recognized the voice of the young police constable. "Over here!" she said.

His skin tone was better, and he sounded a little more comfortable in his role as detective—at least until someone with more authority arrived.

Dodo moved away to give him some privacy with Lady Barchester. He wasn't likely to ask anything she hadn't already thought of but she stayed close enough to hear just in case.

Methodically, the officer went through the timeline of events, asking when Lady—Mrs. Barchester—noticed her husband missing and ending with her finding the body.

"He appears to have been killed with a sharp knife whose blade is about three inches wide," he announced when she was done.

Mrs. Barchester paled again, lips slightly parted.

"We're still looking for the murder weapon," he continued.

A sudden disturbance by the door interrupted the interrogation and a deep, familiar bass thrust its way into the room.

Chief Inspector Blood.

Chapter 4

Before Dodo actually saw the chief inspector, her mouth went dry. A tumble of memories clamored for her attention. They had met at the country house where the maid had been murdered. He had *not* made a good first impression, crashing in like the proverbial bull. In fact, he had been the Darcy to her Elizabeth, rudely dismissing her as an incompetent and bruising her ego. But in the end, he had come to appreciate her value when she helped uncover the murderer, and he had softened.

So had she.

But the fact was that an enormous societal gulf separated them.

Her eyes jumped to the entrance of the box without her permission, the anticipation of seeing the chief inspector kicking her pulse into an annoyingly erratic pattern. When he stepped into the room, she was not surprised to see him wearing the familiar brown trench coat and trilby hat that sat perfectly on his strong head, framing his flaming copper eyes. Dodo could only see his profile at this point, and he looked…tired. Perhaps policemen were always tired.

It was obvious that he still had not seen her as he flashed his credentials at Alistair's parents, asking to see the widow. Mr. Guthrie pointed to Mrs. Barchester and it was only then that the chief inspector spotted Dodo.

As their eyes locked, the chief inspector stopped as abruptly as a train in a head on collision.

A variety of emotions flickered across his features, surprise, pleasure, frustration, resignation. One side of his mouth twitched, and his eyes lit up for a second, like someone striking a match in a dark room.

Dodo felt a warm sunshine spread through her. She had forgotten how ruggedly handsome he was.

"Lady Dorothea." He nodded, keeping his tone professional but holding her gaze as if they were the only two people in the crowded room.

"Come, come Chief Inspector. I believe you have earned the right to call me Dodo."

His burnished brown eyes twinkled.

"Oh, thank goodness you are here," sniffed Mrs. Barchester smashing the connection. The chief inspector cleared his throat and dragged his eyes over to the widow.

"Lady Barchester—"

"It's plain 'Mrs.' now."

It was hard to tell if this fact was a trial or not as her expression was so tight with grief and shock.

"Mrs. Barchester. Let me first offer my condolences." His voice was smooth and silky as he took off his hat in a sign of respect, revealing chestnut brown waves that needed a trim.

Mrs. Barchester attempted to smile but her muscles were already busy with crying.

"I have a few questions…" He pulled a chair over and sat down. He hadn't asked Dodo to leave so she stayed.

"Can you remember what time your husband left this box?"

Mrs. Barchester's face crumpled like a used piece of tissue paper as she concentrated, her hat plumes bouncing with no appreciation for the current crisis.

"It was just before the race at four o'clock. He had won his bet on the previous race and was going to collect his winnings. If only I'd gone with him." Her sodden handkerchief came up again.

"You may have been killed also," Chief Inspector Blood said gently.

The tears stopped as she considered this statement. She shuddered.

"And you discovered the body at fifteen minutes past four?" the chief inspector continued.

"Yes. Honestly, I feel a little out of my league with high society—we are new and don't really fit in. I was feeling awkward here alone and decided to go in search of him."

"Did he win a lot of money on the race? I don't believe we found any cash on him. Could it have been a robbery gone bad?"

That's not the real reason he left.

Mrs. Barchester wiped her shining cheeks. "No. I think it was about thirty pounds. I wondered why he didn't just wait until the end of the day to collect it. We had several more bets placed later."

Dodo cleared her throat and stared hard at the chief inspector. An imperceptible nod indicated that he understood her meaning.

After several more preliminary questions the chief inspector learned that Lord and Lady Barchester really didn't know any of the other guests and the name of the new Lord Barchester.

"Thank you, Mrs. Barchester. That will be all for now. You've had a nasty shock. Would you like an officer to escort you home?" The genuine concern in his tone was like a soft rolling, distant thunder.

"Do you know, I think I would like that, Inspector. I'm a bit numb and my head is spinning." Her eyes were raw as she put her hand up to steady the ridiculous hat.

Chief Inspector Blood beckoned over a constable and explained what was needed.

"Make sure someone stays with her for a few hours."

The ex-Lady Barchester gathered her things and followed the policeman in a trance.

Chief Inspector Blood tipped his head and Dodo followed him over to a quiet corner. He said nothing but his face was full of unblinking expectation.

He was dangerously close.

She reached her hand into the top of her dress under the flutter cape. A hint of shock registered on the chief inspector's face.

"I found this. It was in his pocket."

Understanding dawned but the chief inspector still hadn't spoken. Instead, his expression melted into disapproval.

Oops.

"The constable on the scene seemed so…inexperienced." She hung the shreds of her dignity on the phrase as she handed over the betting stub.

The chief inspector turned it over, then read the handwritten note. The script was childish, sloping, and Dodo was of the opinion that it was probably written with the left hand to disguise it.

"So, he lied to his wife." His tone was back to business. The gruff edge told her he was mad, and it stung. Her stomach dropped.

"It would appear so."

She searched his face to gauge if she should ask forgiveness, noticing a scar on his brow she had never seen before. She idly wondered if it was from his childhood. Did he have siblings?

Under her gaze, the deep eyes softened, and she realized that she was mistaken about his anger. The change in his tone must have been due to the news that Lord Barchester had not been forthcoming with his wife. As if turning to a new page in his mind, he surprised her by asking, "How have you been Lady Dorothea?"

Relief that he wasn't annoyed poured over her. "Very well, thank you."

"Helped with any more murders?" His intonation was uncharacteristically light.

"As a matter of fact—"

He raised a hand. "I don't think I want to know."

Pulling at the tie around his neck as if it was suddenly strangling his Adam's apple, he asked, "What else can you tell me about this murder?"

"Actually, I am a guest here and don't know anyone except Charlie. Who you've met."

The chief inspector's face fell as he cut his gaze over to where Dodo indicated. He pinched his lips and smiled like a cat about to rush a mouse. "Ah, Mr. N.I.C.E."

Dodo scowled. She had described Charlie as 'nice' during the investigation into the maid's death and the chief inspector had mocked the description. "For your information he is more than nice, Chief Inspector. He has been the perfect gentleman."

"High praise indeed," he scoffed.

Dodo cleared her throat. "Moving on. Alistair Guthrie, over there with the flaming hair, is the son of the couple who hired the box for today's races. Alistair knows Charlie from college." The chief inspector nodded as he wrote down the names.

"Colonel and Mrs. Winchester, the older couple over by the food table, are their guests. The colonel is a cabinet member in the current government."

Chief Inspector Blood turned to look, and recognition sparked.

"The four young people seated at the table are guests of Alistair. The angry-looking young woman with the scar is Felicity something and she brought her current beau, Alexander someone or other. He is the reason for her ill temper. Fancies himself a revolutionary. Fascist leanings, I think. The other girl in the polka dots with the light brown curls is Portia with a double-barreled last name, and lastly Roger somebody. They are not together, but I sense that she would like to be."

Chief Inspector Blood chuckled. "Very detailed." He quirked a brow.

"I just met them!" she cried in her defense.

"So, you don't know anyone?"

"Other than Charlie, no."

"What were you two doing when the murder was discovered?"

Dodo feigned shock as if telling him would be embarrassing and she was gratified to see a slight blush under his five o' clock shadow. For some reason she could not help herself from teasing him.

"I mean, where were you?" he clarified.

"We were out on the deck watching the racing. Together."

He hid his face in his notebook. "Anyone else out there with you?"

"I was rather engrossed with Charlie…"

The chief inspector chewed the inside of his mouth as he wrote.

"… but I think most of the others were inside," she continued. "Well, so I assumed, but of course Lord Barchester was not in there and his wife had gone in search of him. Sorry. That makes me a very unreliable witness."

Chief Inspector Blood rolled his neck. "How about any interaction you noticed between the guests earlier?"

"The young people kept to themselves and Lord and Lady Barchester were a little aside… I think she is right that they hadn't been fully accepted yet. But I did see Mrs. Guthrie making an effort to be inclusive."

"You didn't hear anyone arguing?"

"Well, the two young men were constantly debating, but not in the context you mean. The Barchesters seemed to be having words when Charlie and I arrived, and the colonel and his wife were having what looked like a rather intense conversation. Just minor irritations though, if you ask me."

"That doesn't sound very promising. It's always easier to start an investigation when there is obvious bad blood."

"Not positing the theory of a passing stranger, then?" she asked, fighting back a smile.

"I make it a habit to keep an open mind, Lady Dorothea, but it always makes most sense to start with those who were known to the deceased."

She seized upon the moment to shine. "I tend to agree, Chief Inspector." She crossed her legs and adjusted her hat. "Here are some things I *have* picked up that might be useful before you start your questioning. Lancelot Bertram thought he was getting the title but instead it went to Lord Barchester. With him out of the way, the title *does* go to Bertram."

Her hand went to her earring and she noticed his eyes follow her fingers.

"Felicity appears to have had some contact with the deceased at a dinner party which she down-played, begging the question why. And Portia saw Felicity leave the box around the time of the murder. She said she was going to the ladies', but she could be lying. Perhaps she wrote the note? And, what's the story with the scar?"

Dodo stretched her leg, twisting her ankle around to iron out a kink and the chief inspector ran a hand down his face.

"Alistair says he went to see a friend," she continued. "Sally someone." She had the good grace to look sheepish at yet another surname she didn't know. "He was *very* uncomfortable admitting it. Why isn't she here in the box? We should check that alibi. Are you writing all this down, Chief Inspector?" She pointed a slender, bejeweled finger at his pencil which was poised but had stopped making contact with the paper.

He looked down as if surprised and scribbled something.

"Alistair did mention that his mother was bending the minister's ear around that time, but if he left to visit his friend, he does not know if either of them left too. He thinks his father and Mrs. Winchester were eating caviar. Same problem with the timing."

Dodo straightened her sheer cape.

"And there's the obvious problem that Lord Barchester lied to his wife, as you so cleverly deduced, about why he was leaving." She stopped to catch her breath.

"Oh, and according to the constable, the murder weapon was a large knife that has not yet been found." She bit her lower lip and felt her power as he dragged his eyes away from her mouth and back to his notes

"Splendid! That background helps a great deal…even if you were hopeless about the murder itself." A flirty smile played on his lips.

She suddenly felt very hot.

The chief inspector looked around the room and cleared his throat. "Since these are your kind—"

Dodo's eyebrows shot up in amusement. "*My* kind, Chief Inspector?"

He pasted a roguish grin on his tanned face, oozing charisma. Really, if he wasn't a policeman she might be interested.

"You know what I mean. Perhaps you wouldn't mind sitting in again like you did for the murder at Farrington Hall? Your lot speak a different language and it might be helpful."

She let her eyes flare. "Of course, Chief Inspector. I would be more than happy to oblige."

He hesitated and opened and closed his mouth before saying, "I suppose we should begin the interviews, then."

Did he seem disappointed that their time was over or was her ego over-inflated?

He called over the colonel.

"Colonel Winchester, I am sure you are a very busy man—"

"I am," he agreed, eyeing Dodo quizzically, his mutton chops moving up and down as his jaw clenched. The chief inspector offered no explanation for her presence.

"Yes, yes. We will have you out of here as soon as we can."

The colonel harrumphed.

Undeterred, the chief inspector continued. "Did you know the deceased?"

"No." The answer was given with military efficiency.

"You had met neither he nor his wife before this afternoon?"

"No."

"You are a colonel. May I ask when and where you served?"

The colonel sat a little taller. "I began my military service as part of the reinforcements sent after the Third Burmese War under the command of Sir Henry Prendergast. The insurgency was constant, and I spent the better part of seven years over there."

"What year would that have been?" asked the chief inspector.

"'86. I shipped out in 1886. I was just twenty-three at the time. Green around the ears. I was thirty by the time I finally came home. I was wounded in my first tour over there and was sent home to receive medical attention." He lifted his trouser leg to reveal a white ragged scar. "Blasted Burmese villagers did this to me. It was a pretty bad cut and prevented me from walking for some time. Got several medals for bravery, though. Went out as an officer cadet and came back a captain. Not bad, eh?" His eyes twinkled.

"And you eventually rose to the rank of colonel."

"Yes, I spent the next thirteen years in the army, on active duty all over the world, and retired at forty-three. I had a good run, but my health was at risk and it was time to find a wife and settle down." His smile was smug, reminding Dodo of someone who has just pounced on the last cream bun.

"When did you and Mrs. Winchester marry?" The chief inspector's pencil was poised.

"1902. We met at a fundraiser for British Veterans."

"And how did you become a guest here today?"

"I have known the Guthries for years. I served with his father before his death." The colonel folded his arms and stroked his whiskers.

"Were you in the box the entire time?"

"Yes, I've got arthritis and have a devil of a time going up and down stairs, so we stayed put." His face squashed into a cheerless smile.

"Your wife too?"

The colonel blinked hard and looked at the ceiling. "She may have gone to use the ladies'. You can ask her."

"Did you have much interaction with Lord Barchester today?"

He grabbed his chin considering the question. "Not much more than small talk if you must know. Not really my kind of chap."

"Thank you, Colonel. I am sure that you are needed at Whitehall. I know where to find you if I have more questions." He held out his hand for the colonel to shake.

The colonel struggled to his feet. "Indeed. Will you be long with my wife? I really *do* need to get back."

"Just need to ask her a few questions, and then you can both be on your way."

The colonel went over to his wife and whispered in her ear. She walked over and sat in the chair, smiling tightly at Dodo.

"Mrs. Winchester," began the chief inspector. "Your husband said you went to use the facilities this afternoon. What time would that have been?"

Mrs. Winchester sucked in her lips reminding Dodo of the toothless fortune-teller who came to the village carnival each year. She put her hand to her mouth to cover a smile. If old age was a battle, Mrs. Winchester was losing the fight.

"Ooh, now. I didn't really pay attention to the time."

"Perhaps you can remember which race had just been run?" suggested Dodo.

Mrs. Winchester flashed her a hot look of contempt but then her face smoothed. "It was well after the royal race, but I can't remember the others. I'm not a gambler, so I didn't have any reason to pay attention to the race times." She settled her wrinkled hands on her lap.

"What did you think of the Barchesters?" asked the chief inspector.

"Not much if you must know. Lady Barchester was lacking a certain finesse in my opinion. One expects a little more from the nobility." She dropped her voice. "And she needs some advice in the fashion department. Her dress did not fit her style at all."

Considering the awful pink gown and cumbersome hat Mrs. Winchester herself was wearing, Dodo had the thought that people in glass houses should not throw stones.

"So, did you speak to them much?"

"We tried but frankly they were hard to talk to. Her husband—God rest his soul—was a little vulgar. Knew very little of my husband's affairs at Whitehall, very little of politics at all."

Her hat, which was a gaudy pink number with tall ostrich feathers, was a little off center, and she patted it into place.

"Did you notice Lord Barchester leave the box around three forty-five?"

"Is that when he left? No, I didn't. After trying and failing to engage them, I left well enough alone."

Dodo was rankled by her snobbery. She doubted Mrs. Winchester had tried very hard at all.

"And you have known the Guthries for a long time, I understand?"

"Ever since I married. Mr. Guthrie's father was a close friend of my husband's."

"Did you know any of the young people?"

"No. I met them for the very first time today." She nodded to Dodo with a forced smile.

"Did you notice anything else that might be of interest?"

Mrs. Winchester dropped her voice. "I did hear that the girl with the scar left the box late in the afternoon. And the tall dark one she was with was rather rude to the colonel."

The chief inspector pursed his lips.

"Thank you, Mrs. Winchester. You are free to go."

Mrs. Winchester gathered her large handbag and gloves. "The colonel has pressing business with the Prime Minister first thing in the morning, and we did not expect to be at Ascot this late. We shall leave immediately."

She stood and grabbed her husband by the arm, practically dragging him from the room.

"What did you think of them?" whispered the chief inspector, when they had gone out the door.

"The colonel may be the one in the Cabinet, but I would wager that it is Mrs. Winchester that rules the roost."

Chapter 5

After a flurry of activity as the Winchesters left, the next person to be questioned was Mrs. Guthrie. Nothing was relaxed about her, especially not her auburn curls which were now sticking in every direction from beneath her hat. In fact, she reminded Dodo of people who were trying to give up smoking; tense and wild eyed. Her full lips were pulled tight over her prominent teeth.

"Isn't it just awful?" she declared, her expression one of intense agitation, her right leg bouncing up and down uncontrollably.

"How well did you know the deceased?" The chief inspector's direct approach did little to put the poor woman at ease.

She placed her hands on her knee in an apparent attempt to stop it moving. "Not very well at all, as a matter of fact. They were invited to a large dinner party I attended several weeks ago, and I sat next to Lady Barchester. She wasn't even sure which fork to use, if you can believe it, and I took pity on her. She told me how nervous she was of the new life they had been forced into, and I decided to make her my little project." Mrs. Guthrie's lips pulled back and exposed her large bite, looking for all the world like a happy chimpanzee.

"I invited them to a little garden party we had and then decided that Ascot was a perfect training ground—especially since we had reserved a private box." Her eyes were both eager and apprehensive. The woman was a barrel of nerves.

The chief inspector's expression remained as blank as a fresh sheet of paper.

Mrs. Guthrie extended her neck. "I thought with just the Winchesters and us here it would be a bit more intimate. You know, enable her to make some friends, but she didn't seem to hit it off with anyone."

"Did you notice either of them leave the box?"

"I saw Lord Barchester leave because I noticed that his wife seemed opposed to his leaving, but I have racked my brain to see if I remember her leaving and -poof! Nothing." Her leg started bobbing again and her frantic eyes kept darting to Dodo.

"How well do you know the other people here?"

"Well, my son invited friends. Some I know, like Charlie, and others I don't, like Lady Dorothea. I think I have met the friendly young man before but the angry, dark one I have never met...and never care to again." Her lips sank into an ingratiating grimace.

"Oh?" The chief inspector lifted his face.

"He has very bad manners, chief inspector. His mother failed terribly with that boy. So negative. I try not to be around negativity—it's so aging."

Chief Inspector Blood raised his brows.

"It messes with my positive energy. Very aging." She nodded as though everyone felt the same. Dodo coughed to hide a chuckle.

"As for the girls, I know sulky Felicity as she has been to the house before and floats in similar circles but Portia, I do not know at all—though *she* seems like a lovely girl."

"As the hostess, did you happen to notice Lord Barchester talking to any of your guests in particular?"

Mrs. Guthrie was now picking at her dress with fussy fingers, avoiding the chief inspector's eye. "I think Felicity chatted with him. And the colonel. They were both in the military. I have no interest in war after the last one and didn't pay any attention."

"Did your husband spend any time with him?"

She crossed her arms and pointed a finger. "I did tell Arthur about my little project and asked him to make an effort, but he is incorrigible and spent most of the time with the colonel. I thought perhaps that's why Lord Barchester left, actually, since no one was talking to him. I felt rather guilty about it and had determined to make more of an effort when he returned."

"And you yourself, did you ever leave the box?"

"I left before luncheon to powder my nose but have stayed put since to be a good hostess." Her face broke into a devastating smile, which she shone at the chief inspector. Dodo thought it was quite inappropriate given the circumstances.

"Thank you, Mrs. Guthrie. If you would send your husband over."

"I think she's withholding something," commented Dodo, "much too nervous. And I think she likes you."

The chief inspector shuddered.

Mr. Guthrie approached and took a seat. The short man's waistcoat strained as he sat and leaned forward.

"Dashed awful business!" he exclaimed. "I hope the King and Queen don't blame us for this. How will we ever live it down?"

Pretty awful for Lord Barchester too!

"Quite." replied the chief inspector. "How well did you know Lord Barchester?"

"Not at all, really. Violet invited them. New people." His nose scrunched up.

A snob.

His stubby fingers were working themselves into a state and he clasped his hands together. "His wife sat next to mine at a party or some such and she decided to help them along. She's always doing that kind of thing, Violet. Marvelous really, but a man wants to relax in his own box, not make small talk with strangers."

Dodo was liking the little man less and less.

The chief inspector chewed his cheek. "Did you talk to him at all?"

Mr. Guthrie pursed his lips. "I tried. Really. It was slow going I can tell you and after a while I gave up. I had a good long chat with the colonel though. He was friends with my father—known him forever—and he has such interesting tales about his time in the army and now in the government. Fascinating man."

"Did you notice *anyone* having a real conversation with Lord Barchester? A conversation that caused some emotion in him, perhaps?" The chief inspector's tone had become tense.

Mr. Guthrie's mouth puckered as he thought. "Can't say that I did. Just the short chat with the colonel. Mostly he and his wife were looking at the races out of the window or on the balcony, I believe."

"And did you notice he, or his wife leave?"

"No. Neither one. Sorry I cannot be of more service." His chin dipped as his brows rose in an expression that did not look in the least sorry.

"That's all for now," said the chief inspector, a note of despair apparent. "We may need to follow up within the next few days."

"Right-o." The heavy-set man pushed himself to his feet, releasing his buttons from their prison and waddled over to his wife. With her horsey features and his girth, not to mention the difference in their height, they were an unlikely couple.

"Useless," muttered the chief inspector under his breath. Dodo agreed.

Chief Inspector Blood pushed out of his seat and went to have a word with the constable who then spoke to the group of younger people. Dodo watched as they all threw anxious looks at each other and then Alistair stood. The eyes of everyone in the group followed him as he walked over to sit in the interview chair.

Alexander remained defiant and indignant.

He'll be fun to question.

"You are Alistair Guthrie?" began the chief inspector.

Alistair gripped the back of the chair as though it was a lifeline and lowered himself into it.

Nervous like his mother. Perhaps it's just a character trait. Or perhaps it's because of Sally.

"I am, sir," Alistair confirmed.

He was jumpy and couldn't have looked more uncomfortable if his trousers had been full of spiders.

"And all the younger people are here at your invitation?" continued the chief inspector.

"Yes." He cast a nervous glance at Dodo who gave him a smile of encouragement.

The chief inspector softened his voice a little. "Perhaps you can tell me a little about them."

Alistair repeated the things he had told Dodo earlier in the day.

"Have you been romantically involved with any of the young ladies?"

Alistair's skin flushed scarlet. "I say, what has that got to do with anything?"

Dodo stepped in to mend the damage. "I'm sure what the chief inspector means to say is, that in his experience, when there has been some kind of romantic relationship between those present at a crime, it changes the dynamics of the whole investigation. Isn't that right, chief inspector?"

"Ahh, yes. Exactly." He cut his eyes over to Dodo with a slight nod.

The redness began a retreat as Alistair replied, "No. We're just friends. Have always been just friends."

"Thank you for being so candid, Mr. Guthrie."

Dodo's lip curled at the conciliatory tone of the chief inspector.

"Now, a witness has told us that you left the box near the time of the murder. Can you tell us where you went?"

The crimson flush made a swift return, and the young man tipped his head, dropping his gaze to the floor. "If I tell you, can I be sure that you won't tell my parents?" His voice was almost a whisper.

Dodo and Chief Inspector Blood exchanged a quick look. *What exactly is he hiding?*

"Unless it has any bearing on the case, it will be kept quite confidential," the chief inspector assured.

"I did pop out to meet someone—a girl actually."

The chief inspector remained quiet. Dodo had learned that silence was a very useful tool in interrogations.

Alistair hung his head even lower. "She's a barmaid at my local pub. Her name is Sally."

Dodo's eyes flared. Fraternizing with the lower classes was a definite no-no even in modern 1923.

The silence continued.

"I told her about coming to Ascot and she had said how she would love to go one day. She can be very persuasive, and I found myself promising her a ticket—not to the box you understand. I bought her a general ticket and paid for a fancy dress and hat and told her I would sneak out to meet her around four. The plan was to join up with her after, for a night on the town."

"What time precisely did you leave the room?"

"Three fifty. On the dot. I was anxious about meeting her and kept looking at my watch."

I bet you were.

"And did you see either Lord or Lady Barchester leaving?"

He nodded. "I noticed Lord Barchester leaving at three forty-five. I had already begun my time watching. Felicity left shortly after him. I waited for her to get down the stairs then I slipped out. I did not see Lady Barchester. Perhaps she left after me?"

"Did anyone else leave around that time?"

"Like I said, Felicity left shortly after Lord Barchester, but I saw no one else."

Dodo jumped in. "So, your previous testimony about the whereabouts of the Winchesters and your parents...?"

Alistair looked sheepish, like a child who has been caught in a lie by his nanny. "Ah, yes. Well, those things did happen, but well before I left the box."

"So, the fact is that you do not know if the older people were still in the box at the time of the murder because you yourself were not here."

She wasn't the only unreliable witness.

"Uh, yes...correct. Sorry." The bones in his face seemed to sink with shame.

The chief inspector made an indeterminate sort of sound. "We will have to question this, Sally, to ensure that she corroborates your testimony."

"Really?" His face fell farther. "I suppose I see that." He shifted in the chair. "Is that all?" Alistair would not have been more anxious to leave had he been sitting outside the dentist's office awaiting an extraction.

"For now." The chief inspector tipped his head towards the policeman in uniform causing the front of his hair to fall across his eyes like a curtain. He pushed it back. "Please give Sally's details to the constable."

As he left, Dodo remarked, "Well, that was a surprise!"

Felicity was heading over to them. Mrs. Guthrie had used the adjective 'sulky' to describe her and it fit. She walked with her face inclined at an unnatural angle, so that her hair formed a veil that hid the scar. As she sat, her blond locks swung back, and the nasty blemish was revealed for a moment before she put her hand up to her cheek.

"Felicity Snodgrass?"

Dodo found it interesting that Felicity's expression improved as the chief inspector leveled his earthy brown eyes on her.

"Yes."

The chief inspector asked general questions and then, "You were seen leaving the box around three forty-five."

Felicity's guard slammed back up with the force of a prison cell door. "I went to use the ladies'. That's not a crime is it?"

Dodo thought she could be a very pretty girl if she dropped the attitude.

"Did you see anyone else on the stairs?"

"I assume you mean from the party? Yes, I was just behind Lord Barchester as it happens."

"Did you see where he went?" asked the chief inspector.

"The ladies' toilets are over by the betting area, and he went the other way."

That corroborates what we already know.

"Did you happen to see exactly where he went?"

Dodo leaned forward.

"No. Why would I?" Felicity's voice had risen, and her tone had an edge to it.

Dodo thought the intensity of the response was excessive.

"No reason, except that you were one of the few people who had met Lord Barchester before today."

Felicity dropped her hand to straighten her dress, taking her time to respond. "He was at a dinner party I attended. I wouldn't call that *knowing* him. He was just one of the other guests. I don't believe we even spoke that day."

"Who was hosting the dinner party?" asked Dodo.

Felicity flashed her an icy glare. "Lord and Lady Carrington-Blythe."

The chief inspector wrote that down. Dodo knew the couple fairly well and thought she could offer to question them about the event given that they were *her* people.

"What about the Winchesters? Do you know them?"

"Someone told me he is in the government or something. I have never met them before."

Chief Inspector Blood shifted in his chair and his expression lost the hard edges. "I hope you don't mind me asking but how did you get that scar?"

Felicity's hand shot up to cover it again and her eyes shadowed. "It has nothing to do with this."

"I am sure it doesn't. I'm just asking as one human being to another."

Dodo doubted that was true.

"I…I had a run in with a horse."

The scar did bear the shape of part of a horseshoe.

"I am so sorry to hear that," the chief inspector replied. "You have such a lovely face—I hope that when it is healed it will be less noticeable."

The indignance drained out of Felicity's face like the tide from the shore. "Me too," she whispered.

Attraction skipped up Dodo's spine at the chief inspector's tender tone. He had used it on her once.

"That is all for now," he continued. "The constable will take down your details—address and telephone number."

The girl that stood was in sharp contrast to the girl that had sat down just moments ago. As she went back to her seat, Felicity cast a lingering look at the chief inspector. He had made a convert.

An uncomfortable emotion was uncurling in Dodo.

Chapter 6

With a petulant scowl Alexander scraped back his chair and walked over to Chief Inspector Blood. He sat, legs stretched out, slouched so low his shoulders almost touched the back of the chair. Mrs. Guthrie was right about his mother.

"You are Alexander Babcott, and you are here with Miss Snodgrass?" The chief inspector's tone was all business again.

"I don't know anyone. I should have been allowed to leave ages ago." The depth of his glower increased.

The chief inspector leveled his gaze at the ill-mannered young man. "I am in charge here, and everyone must be questioned."

Alexander growled. It was most unattractive.

"How do you know Miss Snodgrass?"

"I met her at a party in London about six months ago." He ran a hand through loose, ebony curls that had fallen into his eyes.

"And she invited you here where you know no one."

"I already told you that."

"Sir." The chief inspector's mouth was set in a grim line.

"What?" Alexander scrunched up his nose.

"I've already told you that, 'sir'." The chief inspector's fingers were gripping his notebook so tightly the knuckles were white.

Alexander's round eyes narrowed to slits. Dodo was fast losing patience with this angry, privileged, young man and his lack of respect for authority.

"What did you think of the afternoon? Did you enjoy the races? Did you win anything?" The chief inspector's tempo had increased.

"I didn't bet today. On principle. It was the royal race, and I believe that the monarchy is an outdated institution."

The chief inspector hid an incredulous grin by dragging his finger across his upper lip.

Enough is enough! Time to put the fellow in his place.

"Isn't your grandmother *Lady* Tadcaster?" asked Dodo with as much fake innocence as she could muster. She had asked Felicity about it after she had mentioned it earlier.

The chief inspector's finger came up again. Alexander shifted in his seat.

"Doesn't mean I'm proud of the fact," bit back Alexander.

The chief inspector pushed his brim up with the end of his pencil and his jaw clenched. "Did you see Lord Barchester leave the box?"

"Why would I care what Lord Barchester is doing?"

The chief inspector pushed back his chair and let out a sigh that was heavy with impatience.

Really, Alexander was pushing the limits. "The chief inspector did not ask you if you *cared* about Lord Barchester," said Dodo, "he asked you if you had noticed him *leave*."

Alexander shot her a withering look. "No, I did not notice the old codger leave."

"Did you observe *anyone* exit the box after the royal race?" barked the chief inspector.

"No." Hostility was rippling off him.

Dodo pounced. "What about Felicity?"

Without moving his head, Alexander shifted his eyes to the side in thought. "Yes, I think she left to visit the ladies'."

"What time was that?" asked the chief inspector.

"No idea."

Questioning Alexander was like swimming in mud.

"Did you see anything unusual this afternoon?" persisted Chief Inspector Blood.

"No." Alexander crossed his arms tightly against his chest.

"I am at a loss to understand why you chose to attend today, Mr. Babcott, if everything about the event is offensive to you," said the chief inspector. "You seem to have wasted your day observing nothing, which makes you a very unreliable witness." This expert shot at the insolent young man's pride found its mark and Alexander squirmed with indignation.

"I'm plenty observant if I need to be," he spat back.

"We'll have to take your word on that, won't we Mr. Babcott?" The chief inspector was a tight spring of frustration.

"That's all for now, but we will probably have more questions later. Go and ask Miss Bodwyn-Jones to come over."

Alexander did as he was bid with the grim smile of a victor, as the chief inspector remarked, "What a thoroughly unlikeable fellow. Don't know what she sees in him."

A curl of jealousy unwound in Dodo's chest. "She's not much more pleasant herself. I think they are well suited."

Portia sat down with a smile that lit up her whole face. Then as she slowly looked back and forth between Dodo and the chief inspector, she seemed to remember that someone had been murdered and rearranged her mobile features appropriately.

"It's just terrible," she declared. "Who would want to kill Lord Barchester? Apart from the title, he was a no one." She made a good point.

"Did you speak to him at all today?" the chief inspector began.

"As a matter of fact, I did try. I knew that he was quite new to his title and had been a working man before. Alistair told me. I appreciate how hard society can be so I thought I would try to strike up a conversation, you know, try to put him at ease." She shook back her honey-colored curls. "It was like pulling teeth even for me. He seemed pre-occupied. Kept asking me to repeat the same question. I gave up after a while."

"What about Lady Barchester?"

"Oh, she was much nicer. Really trying to fit in. I suppose it's all to no avail now as the title will move on to the next in line."

"I understand that to be the case," said the chief inspector. "Did any of the other people try to talk to him?"

"Obviously, Alistair carried on some small talk with him as the son of the hosts. I saw Mr. Guthrie talk to him for a bit, but he gave up too. And I think Felicity talked to him a little, but the three other men didn't seem to make any kind of effort. Oh, no I'm wrong." She looked at Dodo with a small smile. "Your friend Charlie—he spoke to him for a while."

The chief inspector cleared his throat. "What about the Winchesters? Did he have any interaction with them?"

Portia tipped back her head. "Hmmm. I remember he and the colonel talking—that was after the colonel sat at our table before his wife told him off. It wasn't a long conversation and I saw the colonel shaking his head a great deal."

Portia was a wealth of information.

"Did you see Lord Barchester leave?"

"I did actually. I had gone back to get some more cakes and he stepped out right then. He was humming to himself."

"Did you see anyone leave right before or immediately after Lord Barchester?"

"Felicity left about that time – call of nature." She blushed. "I don't remember seeing anyone else…Perhaps Mrs. Guthrie? But that could have been earlier. I wasn't paying all that much attention as Roger is such good company." Her expression radiated hope.

"And you yourself had not met Lord Barchester before today?"

Her full lips pulled down in disappointment. "No, sorry. I'm not much help."

"On the contrary. You have been most helpful." Portia's shoulders came up and she squirmed with delight.

"If you think of anything else please give me a call." The chief inspector pulled a card from his jacket pocket and handed it to Portia.

"Now, if you wouldn't mind sending over Mr. Farnsworth?"

"Of course."

"Marvelous witness," exclaimed the chief inspector as Portia walked away. "Wish more people were like that."

"Is that a dig at me, Chief Inspector?"

"Oh no." The chief inspector turned to her with a raw, earnest expression. "I didn't mean to imply—"

Dodo fought back a smile. "I was just teasing you. I happen to agree. First class."

Roger walked purposefully over and sat down, his boutonniere looking the worse for wear.

"Mr. Farnsworth?"

"Yes, sir."

Respect at last. Dodo had no complaints against *his* mother.

"What do you think of all this?" The chief inspector waved his hand around vaguely.

"What? The murder? Dreadful, sir. Simply awful." He reminded Dodo of an old garden fence, sturdy but in need of some touch up. Though not traditionally handsome, he did exude a certain presence, a charisma that drew one to him. Dodo could see why Portia was interested.

"Just as well the King and Queen had already left, what?" His brows formed a question. "Did you see anything during the afternoon that might have hinted at problems?" asked the chief inspector.

"Not really. I tried to strike up a conversation about the weather with him while I was at the food table, as one does. Bit hard to engage. Reminded me of my father, actually." Roger gave a guilty smile. "Didn't pay him much attention after that."

"Miss Felicity appears to have known him," said the chief inspector.

"Really? I didn't realize." Roger had a pale sprinkling of freckles across his nose that Dodo had not noticed previously.

"She didn't mention it?" asked the chief inspector.

"Not that I heard. But now that you suggest it – I did see her looking his way a couple of times, though who can blame her being tired of Alex?" The left side of Roger's lips hitched with contempt.

"Care to elaborate?"

"It's fun to debate for a bit, but Alexander doesn't seem to know when to stop. Always swinging for a fight. I noticed Felicity looking over in Lord Barchester's direction. I thought she was just weary of the debating, but maybe it was deliberate, and I misread her?"

The chief inspector wrote something in the ubiquitous black notebook.

"Did you see anyone leave the box between three forty-five and four fifteen?"

Roger pursed his lips in thought. "I think Felicity left to powder her nose. I've been up here all afternoon, myself. Portia is a fascinating girl. I was just thinking of visiting the gents when…well, when we heard the screaming." He glanced from the chief inspector to Dodo for validation.

"Lady Barchester must have left. You didn't see her leave, perhaps?"

He colored. "No. Frankly, I was all wrapped up with the young people and the races by that point." His lower lip dragged down in apology. "Won quite nicely on the three-fifteen." He grinned and then noticing the wilting boutonniere, tried to pull it up, but it stubbornly refused and drifted back to its former inebriated position.

"Well, thank you for your time," said the chief inspector, standing. "We'll probably be in touch again."

Roger rose and the chief inspector raised his voice. "Thank you, ladies and gentlemen. You are now free to leave. Expect a follow up from us in the next few days."

Charlie headed toward them, hand extended. "Hello again," he said with a smile. "No hard feelings, Chief Inspector."

Dodo cast the chief inspector an 'I told you so!' look. Charlie was able to bury the hatchet, unlike so many men whose manhood had been threatened. The two men had last met at Farrington Hall when the maid had been murdered and the chief inspector had considered Charlie a suspect.

The two men shook hands. The chief inspector was at least twelve years older than Charlie and though Charlie certainly had the advantage in the looks department there was just something about Chief Inspector Blood that awakened an interest in Dodo that Charlie failed to. Perhaps it was the fact that the chief inspector was untouchable.

"Did you want to question *me*?" Charlie's brow was raised in query.

"No need. Lady Dorothea assures me that you and she were together the whole time and were out on the balcony when the body was discovered."

"That is true, yes."

Charlie turned his gaze to Dodo. "Can we go?"

Dodo looked back to check with the chief inspector.

"My constables will have questioned those near where the body was found to see if they saw anything or anyone that might give us a lead." He popped the notebook in his pocket. "But before you go, I do want to ask if you have any theories, m'lady."

Though his tone was friendly, it bothered Dodo that he used the deferential phrase. It threw up a wall between them that stung. More than once she had asked him to call her Dodo. However, she was gratified that he was seeking her opinion. "I appreciate you asking, Chief Inspector. I just thought of some questions that need answering, really. Who gave Lord Barchester the note? Why did he not tell his wife about it? How well did Felicity *really* know him?"

"I'd say that was the long and short of it at this point," agreed the chief inspector. "Along with, where is the murder weapon?"

"Ah, I have a rather grisly theory on that," announced Charlie, his face suddenly serious. They both looked at him. "I went to carve some beef a little before three-thirty and the knife was gone. I didn't think much of it at the time. I found an ordinary knife and hacked some off. But look." All eyes went to the food table where the beef carving knife was clearly visible. "It's back." Charlie shuddered.

Dodo was hit by a wave of utter repulsion.
How diabolical! How cold-blooded!
A sudden realization hit her. *If that* was *the murder weapon,* t*here could be little doubt that s*omeone *who had been in the room with them was the murderer.*

Chief Inspector Blood let out a dull groan before striding over to the beef roast. Taking out a handkerchief, he picked up the knife and examined it. "Looks about the correct blade size and it's certainly sharp enough." He swung back around, the knife in his hand. "What time did you say it was missing?"

"I came to carve some beef at around three-thirty. But I couldn't say how long before that it had been missing." Charlie dragged the back of his hand across his mouth.

"That changes our timeline though, Mr. Chadwick. I had assumed that the murderer followed Lord Barchester out but this observation switches that around. The murderer could have exited the box *before* Lord Barchester and laid in wait for him at the meeting place."

"Oh, Charlie! That is a marvelous clue. Well done!" cried Dodo, her stomach still a touch queasy.

Catching the chief inspector's expression, she noticed that he looked suddenly crestfallen. Or did she flatter herself?

Charlie, on the other hand, looked like a schoolboy who was bringing home an A grade after a whole term of D's.

"Constable," said the chief inspector raising his voice again. "Can you find me a bag for this knife?"

The constable hurried away to fulfill the commission.

Chief Inspector Blood turned back to them. "Do you happen to know the Carrington-Blythes?" A more vulnerable version of the chief inspector was now on display.

"Yes, actually I do. I was going to mention it," she said.

"I tend to ruffle the feathers of the well-to-do, as you know." His tone was self-deprecating which made her heart beat a little faster in her chest. "Would you be able to ask them about the dinner party that Felicity and the Barchesters attended?"

"I think I might be persuaded to do that for you, Chief Inspector."

"Where can I reach you?" New lines around his eyes indicted worry.

"She's staying with us," intercepted Charlie. "At my parent's house. It's local so it was convenient for the races today."

The chief inspector's expression dropped faster than a penny in a pond. "If I need you, I will call the Chadwick residence. You know where to contact me," he added.

Dodo nodded.

Charlie took her hand and led her to the door. Just as they were stepping through, she tossed a glance backward to find the chief inspector still, knife in hand, staring after her.

Chapter 7

It had been a long day and Dodo was exhausted. She and Charlie sneaked into the basement kitchen when they reached the Chadwick manor to ferret out a snack before calling it a night. The family must have had Victoria sponge for dinner. One of her favorites.

"Funny that it's old Blood again," said Charlie, tearing off a piece of baguette he found in the bread bin.

Dodo poked around looking for the cake.

"Yes, I suppose it is," she murmured, lifting various china plates and lids.

"I wonder how many detectives Scotland Yard has?" Charlie was now hacking off a chunk of English farmhouse cheddar. Having failed to find any remnants of the Victoria sponge, Dodo turned her attentions to the cheese. Another favorite.

"No idea. Cut me off a piece!"

When a child finds their birthday presents early, there is a particular smile of triumph. That was the smile that crept across Charlie's face.

"What?" she said, with a frown.

"I might demand a payment."

Guessing his intentions, she approached like a cat and placed a kiss on Charlie's cheek. "Now can I have a piece?"

He slid the knife through the pale yellow, crumbly cheese and offered the slice to her on the blade. The rich odor made her mouth water. She opened her lips and Charlie slid the knife into her mouth. Her tastebuds exploded.

Charlie's eyes fixed on the bare knife. "Fancy the murderer using the carving knife to kill the poor chap."

The cheese hit her stomach with a thud.

As she contemplated the fact that someone had brazenly swiped the meat carver, plunged it into Lord Barchester's back and then callously replaced it in the roast for all the guests to use, her insides rolled and hunger fled.

"Charlie!" she complained. "I did not need to be reminded of that."

"Sorry, old thing! It was seeing this knife." He dropped it onto the wooden table.

"I've lost my appetite," she said, rubbing her abdomen.

"Then let me escort you to your room. It's the least I can do." His cravat was untied and hanging loosely around his neck. He looked good.

They left the kitchen and crept into the front hall that was dark with shadows, giggling their way up the stairs. At her door he leaned against the frame.

"Excluding the unfortunate turn of events at the end, did you enjoy your day?"

"Yes! It was marvelous! Thank you."

He hesitated but she did not lean forward. Time to set expectations. She wasn't ready to move forward just yet.

"Tomorrow, I will call the Carrington-Blythes and set up a time to question them about their dinner party."

"Oh," said Charlie, stepping back slightly. "Of course. Splendid idea."

He placed a gentle kiss on her cheek. "Good night then."

He is rather sweet.

"Good night, Charlie." She turned to open the door and then looked over her shoulder at him. "And thanks again. I had a really lovely time."

His face broke into a smile of resignation and he lifted his hand and moved into the shadows.

Dodo fell asleep almost immediately but wrestled all night with nightmares involving knives, roast beef and the King.

***

She awoke feeling worse than when she had gone to bed. Today would require some extra time on make-up.

She dressed simply in a creamy linen skirt and blush lace blouse, wrapping a scarf around her head with the help of a Chadwick maid. Delicate, pink, pearl earrings and pearlescent lipstick, finished the look.

After a light breakfast, she asked permission to use the telephone. Charlie had still not appeared.

She found her way to the dark, oak telephone cabinet that smelled of lemon oil. "The Carrington-Blythe residence, Kingston-upon Thames 225, please," she said into the mouthpiece.

Dodo could hear the operator slotting in various plugs. "You're through," sang the voice at the other end.

"Carrington-Blythe residence," said a rather young sounding butler.

"Good morning. I'm sorry to call so early." She eyed the time. It was ten o' clock in the morning, early for her mother. "I wonder if I could leave a message for Lady Carrington-Blythe?"

"Her ladyship is up if you would like to talk to her?"

"Really? Oh, that would be splendid."

"Whom may I say is calling?"

"Lady Dorothea Dorchester."

"Very good, m'lady."

The butler laid down the earpiece and Dodo waited, still surprised that Victoria Carrington-Blythe was not lounging in bed. Dodo had decided on a ploy during breakfast.

"Dodo darling," came the breathy sound of Lady Victoria down the line. "It's simply marvelous to hear from you." An image of the woman smothered in chiffon as gauzy as her voice, came to mind.

"Look, I'm sorry to call so early…"

"Nonsense, darling! I'm always up at the crack of dawn. Suffer terribly from insomnia these days. Getting old is not for the faint of heart."

"You sound like my mother," chuckled Dodo.

"How is dear Guinevere?"

"Very well, thank you. Look, I'm staying at Chadwick Hall. I came down for the races yesterday, and wondered if I might swing by for tea today since I'm on your side of the Thames?"

"Oh darling, I have a tennis lesson this afternoon with Vladimir."

Dodo idly wondered if tennis wear came in chiffon.

"Oh well, would any other time work before I leave?"

"How about lunch? It's just me and Barty today. Nothing formal you understand."

"Lunch would be splendid!" replied Dodo with relief. Time was of the essence in murder investigations. "Can I bring someone? Charlie?"

"Of course, dear. We eat around twelve-thirty."

"See you then." Dodo replaced the receiver.

Part one accomplished.

***

Charlie had been eager to attend the luncheon. He had finally appeared at eleven, profuse with apologies but dressed impeccably and ready for the day. He had chosen tennis whites with a navy cravat. Yummy. And perfect for an informal lunch.

They were now waiting in the Carrington-Blythe drawing room which was decorated in the French style. Her mother would love it. Her own tastes ran to more modern décor.

"Darlings," said Lady Carrington-Blythe as she drifted in on an aroma of hibiscus.

They both stood and she barreled towards them with kisses. "Sit, sit."

Looking from one to the other with a knowing eye, she beamed. "It is so lovely to see you, Dodo. It's been an absolute age!"

"So generous of you to have us at such short notice, Lady Carrington-Blythe," said Charlie. "Dodo was dying to see you since we were in Windsor."

He really does have the most charming manners.

"Nonsense!" she declared. "And do call me Victoria. I love spending time with the young. I spend far too much time with people my own age and let me tell you, they can be quite depressing and serious." She opened a fan and waved it by her face. Her girth meant that she was often over-heated. "We will have lunch on the small patio. Does that suit?"

"I love eating al fresco," replied Dodo.

"Barty will meet us out there." Bartholomew Carrington-Blythe was Lady Victoria's second husband. In both proportions and temperament, they were very well-suited.

The butler appeared like an apparition. "Luncheon is served, m'lady."

They all followed him out to a beautiful patio on the west side of the manor house. It was fashioned out of pastel flagstones and had a black, wrought iron table with matching chairs. It was nicely shaded at this time of day and looked onto a large fishpond with a little bridge across the middle and a fountain in the front.

"What a lovely spot," remarked Charlie.

"I simply love to sit here in the afternoons in the summer. Very relaxing." Lady Victoria allowed the butler to seat her and they followed suit. As he left to fetch their lunch, Barty burst through the glass doors.

"Hello, hello!" he bellowed. "Please excuse my tardiness. Was just on the phone with my mother. Couldn't get the old dear to take the hint that I had to go."

"I am surprised your mother will talk to you on the telephone," remarked Dodo, lifting her hand to allow Barty Carrington-Blythe to kiss it. "*My* mother still hates the thing. She calls it a 'contraption'."

"My mother is eighty-five and is absolutely fascinated by the telephone. Can you imagine what life was like in 1839 when she was born? She views the telephone as a miracle and calls me almost every day. She also has a penchant for fast motor cars."

"She sounds delightful," pronounced Charlie.

"She's a character, that's for sure," Lord Barty replied.

The butler reappeared with two manservants, both balancing platters and plates. An enormous filet of smoked salmon smiled up at Dodo. It was one of her favorites.

"Dig in!" commanded Lady Victoria. "No standing on ceremony here."

Charlie flashed Dodo a smile of contentment and she felt her heart catch.

Good. Something was happening.

Though Dodo was eager to get to the matter in hand, they spent time catching up on family matters and life milestones before

Lady Victoria fortuitously changed the topic. "I say, were you two at the races yesterday when the murder occurred?"

"As a matter of fact, we were," said Dodo, swiping another piece of the delicious fish to go with the shrimp vol-au-vents and crusty English bread. "Would you believe we were actually in the same party as the victim?"

Hook landed.

"Oh, my dears. How perfectly dreadful." Her words did not match her expression, which was more akin to a child beholding gifts under the tree on Christmas morning.

Here was Dodo's opening. "Do you know Lord and Lady Barchester?"

"We do! We had a dinner party not four weeks ago and he was invited as a new peer. We try to do our part to be inclusive. It makes me shudder to think that the poor man is now dead." Her crimson lips pulled down into a frown.

"Not a natural in the position of Earl," remarked Barty, wiping his mouth with a pink serviette. "Rather hard to talk to as I recall. But his wife, she made more of an effort. Until the 'thing'. Wouldn't you agree Victoria?"

Dodo and Charlie shared a look of confusion.

Thing?

"Yes, she was a little over-eager if I recall. It must be very difficult to elbow your way into society rather than be born to it, and the gentry can be so harsh. I believe she told me that her father was a banker—not even a banker in the City but a small-town bank manager. She was going to have a hard time being accepted as it was, without the 'incident'."

"Incident?" asked Dodo, her pulse kicking up a notch.

Victoria cut her eyes over to her husband. She couldn't resist sharing a little gossip, as Dodo knew very well.

"Yes. It caused some tension. Lady Barchester couldn't find her husband for a while—I expect she felt the need for his support—and went to look for him with no success. He eventually came in, trailed by a young woman, and Lady Barchester let him have it. Not very discreet, if I may offer an opinion. He told her to calm down and not cause a scene and she shut up, but not before most everyone in the room noticed. Not the best way to go about being accepted."

Dodo speared a buttery, boiled potato. "Why was she so angry?"

"I believe she accused him…" Lady Victoria paused for dramatic effect, "of messing around with the girl."

Dodo's fork hovered, suspended. "Messing around?"

"Yes! She was a sullen little thing with a nasty gash on her cheek. Felicia…Phillipa…"

Charlie and Dodo locked eyes.

"Felicity?" asked Dodo.

"Yes! That's it! Felicity. Lady Barchester got quite uppity and started to say some things before her husband shut her down. They left soon after. Caused quite a stir. Everyone loves a bit of a scandal."

"Accused him of canoodling," added Barty, stroking his elaborate moustache.

"Did he know Felicity?" asked Charlie, leaning forward.

"The way I heard it," began Lady Victoria, sipping from her cocktail, "he had gone outside for some air and she was out there crying. He had offered a bit of sympathy and one thing lead to another…"

Dodo expelled a sharp breath. Lord Barchester and Felicity? Her mind reeled.

"What was she crying about?" Dodo asked, the potatoes forgotten.

"Something to do with some chap and the cut on her face." Lady Victoria snapped her fingers and one of the manservants refilled her glass.

"Do you know how Felicity got the scar?" asked Charlie, rapt with attention.

"I asked about that after Felicity left. I was curious. They say"—she paused again—"that her young man did it to her." She leaned back, lips tight, eyes narrowed.

"He hit her?" cried Charlie.

"Oh no! Nothing of that kind. I believe they were out riding, and he lost control of his horse while she had dismounted, and it bucked and clipped her on the cheek. Could have been a lot worse, if you ask me. She's lucky she wasn't disfigured or even killed. By all accounts he wasn't suitably sympathetic."

"I can well imagine," said Dodo, folding her napkin.

Lady Victoria's head snapped up. "You know them?"

Dodo thought it wouldn't hurt to reward Lady Victoria with some information in return. "Not really, but as it happens, Felicity and her fellow were members of the party at the races yesterday too."

"Well, well, well," said Barty, blowing out his cheeks. "That's a bit of a coincidence."

"It is rather," agreed Dodo. She didn't like coincidences in murder investigations.

"Tell us all about it," said Lady Victoria with undisguised eagerness, her fingers wiggling.

Dodo, with helpful comments from Charlie, told their hosts everything about meeting the King and Queen at Ascot and the party in the box, including the detail about the mysterious note, ending with the discovery of the body. She withheld their part in finding the victim and helping the chief inspector.

"And Felicity is the only one seen leaving the room around the same time?" Lady Victoria was leaning so far forward she almost ate the floral centerpiece as she spoke. "That seems rather suspicious."

"But why would she murder him? I would expect them to have a romantic rendezvous if anything," pointed out Barty.

"Perhaps he was breaking it off with Felicity because of his wife," declared Lady Victoria. "In desperation Felicity plunged the knife into his back as he left her."

"If she took the knife that would suggest pre-meditation," offered Charlie, sipping lemonade. "What you are suggesting is a crime of passion."

Lady Victoria slumped back in her chair. "Blast! You're right."

"What about Lady Barchester?" suggested Barty. "Perhaps she suspected something, slipped the knife into her handbag, and followed them. When she saw Felicity leave the box, she assumed they were meeting up and followed them. Furious at his infidelity, she plunged the knife into her husband in a fit of jealousy—a woman scorned and all that—and then pretended to find the body by screaming, after hiding the knife back in her handbag."

As he theorized something clicked in Dodo's mind. She pictured Lady Barchester leaning over the body of her husband.

There was no bag in her hand.

Chapter 8

The Surrey countryside sped past them as they returned from the Carrington-Blythe's. The image of Lady Barchester leaning over her husband was like a train waiting at the station, it would not leave Dodo's mind. But the new knowledge that she and her husband had engaged in a public contre-temps at a dinner party a few weeks before, threw new light on the lady's statement that she had followed her husband because she felt out of place with strangers. What if she *had* seen Felicity leave and jumped to the conclusion that another illicit rendezvous was at hand?

"Dodo? Did you hear me?" Charlie was asking her a question and she had not heard his previous one at all.

"I'm sorry. My head is in the clouds." She flashed him a pout.

A smile split his face. "There's a pretty park close to here. Want to make a pit stop?"

She touched his arm. "That sounds lovely."

He took a turn off the main road and within five minutes they were at a park with an attractive large pond complete with ducks and swans, a white pergola, and wandering footpaths.

Romantic.

Charlie came round to open the door and taking her hand, helped her out. The smell of honeysuckle floated in the air. Charlie kept hold of her hand and asked if it was alright without saying a word. She smiled and nodded. There was so much about Charlie to like.

"So, that was a bit of a surprise, what?" he said.

"You mean the Barchesters having a public disagreement?" Dodo replied.

"Actually, I was thinking of the fact that Felicity and he had some kind of romantic connection." His expression telegraphed his incredulity.

Dodo pictured the dead man. He was in his fifties, with a full head of gray hair and a slightly heavy middle. Not particularly attractive. "I know. It is hard to believe. Perhaps he just showed her sympathy when she was at her most vulnerable. I wonder exactly what she was crying about?"

"That fool of a chap Alexander, probably. And *he* is the cause of that awful gash on her face. I'm surprised she's still with him."

"It was just a horrible accident. Perhaps he's filled with guilt about it and is very solicitous of her."

"Does that sound like him?" Charlie kicked a rock.

"No. Perhaps we should visit Felicity and ask her about that night?"

"Do you think she will talk to us? She's rather moody."

A young child ran by chasing a duck with some bread and Charlie moved her hand to the crook of his arm to make way.

"We'll never know if we don't try. And anyway, I think she likes you. I can't say the same for myself."

"What? You don't like me?" A jester's smile lit up his handsome face, his eyes twinkling.

She playfully slapped him. "I meant Felicity. She doesn't like *me*."

"I can see why. Until you showed up, she was the prettiest girl in the room. Even with the scar."

Dodo stopped walking.

"Do you really think that? About me, I mean."

Charlie turned to face her. "Of course, I mean it. Can't you tell I'm crazy about you? You are one of the most beautiful young women I know, and I keep pinching myself that you are actually here with me." Charlie's eyes matched the perfect blue of the sky.

Dodo was touched. She tried not to be vain, but she also tried hard to impress, and it was satisfying to know that it was working. She suddenly realized that Charlie's eyes had slipped to her lips. Her heart flipped over, and she leaned in halfway.

He pressed his soft lips against hers.

Nothing.

The kiss was perfect but there was no spark of connection. On her side anyway. She opened one eye but his were closed, drinking in the moment with undisguised pleasure. Clearly, he was feeling electricity. And the moment could not be more perfect—the sun, the park, the trees…the handsome man…but she just wasn't as moved as she had hoped to be, desperately wanted to be. She closed her eye again and tried to sink into the moment.

It was no good.

When Charlie pulled away, he met her gaze with a hunger in his eyes. Something had changed in him. She knew that look. He was allowing himself to fall in love with her.

What should I do?

Her mind kicked into full power mode and she sifted through her options. Here was a perfectly kind, attractive man from her own set who was offering her his heart. Any girl would be over the moon to be his sweetheart—and she felt herself lucky—but she worried about the morality of leading him on if she didn't have romantic feelings for him. Her thoughts went to her own mother who had married her father while admitting that she was not really in love with him at the time. Her love had grown. Grown into something deep, lasting, and beautiful. Perhaps it would be the same for her with Charlie? And she did have a bad track record of choosing chumps. Charlie was no chump.

All this logic and reasoning happened in the space of a mere second. She looked into Charlie's eyes. They were soft and brimming with desire and hope. His tender look dissolved her doubts, and she came to a decision. She was going to give him a chance to win her heart. Just as her mother had done with her father.

"I really like you Dodo." He ran his finger along her cheek, and it tickled pleasantly.

"I like you too." It wasn't a lie. She *did* like him. Everybody liked him. He was so nice. As the word entered her mind, an image of Chief Inspector Blood appeared, and she swatted it away.

"I'd like to see you more this summer. Spend some time together. See where this takes us."

"Me too."

He cupped her face in his hands and placed sweet kisses on her forehead, cheeks, and then her lips. It was very pleasant but again, that jolt of attraction was missing.

I just need to give it time.

"I've actually always had a thing for you," he confessed, dipping his head and looking up at her. His eyes were deep pools reflecting his strong emotions.

She narrowed her eyes. "Really? Even when I was a bit of an ugly duckling?"

"You were never really—"

Dodo held up a hand to stop him. "If we are going to have a relationship I must insist on honesty. I most definitely *was* an ugly duckling."

He chuckled. "Okay. I'm not going to comment on that. But since you were sixteen, I have always hoped…"

"I am flattered Mr. Chadwick." And she was.

"When you paired up with Julian Jeffries during the weekend at Farrington Hall, I was devastated. I had big hopes for that weekend."

"And you see how well that worked out!" she cried.

Julian had been arrested for killing someone in a hit and run. The memory of her humiliation came roaring back.

"Yes. I tried not to rejoice in that. Failed. But I tried."

She felt his thumb brush hers.

Charlie took her hand again and they continued their promenade around the small lake, past a weeping willow that brushed the path in front of them.

"Tell me about your work with fashion."

Dodo happily filled him in on how she had started to work for Renée Dubois in Paris and how that, in turn, led to her work with British fashion.

"I feel like I'm miles behind you in the real world," he remarked. "College delays adulthood in many ways."

"Do you still want to be a college professor?" He had mentioned this during the weekend at the Farrington's and she had not been able to align his fun, easy-going personality with such a stodgy profession.

"I waiver back and forth. You know I love to travel and if I could find another career that allowed me to indulge in that, I would dive in headlong. The long summers are what attract me to a professorship."

"I must confess, I still can't see you in that role," she said. "Have you considered the military?"

He took a deep breath and guided her to a bench. "That would certainly involve travel, but I wouldn't be in control of where and I wouldn't be free to explore."

A snow-white swan glided past, it's long neck tall and graceful.

"Ah, that's true."

A thought suddenly hit her. "I can't remember where Lord Barchester served. I'm sure it was mentioned."

Charlie's face creased in concentration. "I think it was in the Far East or something."

"How do you know?"

"Someone heard him talking to Colonel Winchester about it and mentioned something at lunch. It caught my attention because it's on my wish list of places to go."

"Can you remember who said it?"

A puff of breeze moved his hair as his brow furrowed. "Is it important?"

"I'm not sure but I'm learning that even the smallest details can be of the utmost importance in solving crime."

Charlie tipped back his head as he thought. "It was not Felicity, I'm sure. Perhaps Portia?"

"Yes, she is a very observant girl. I'd like to know more details about it. Let's set up a tea with her and find out."

"And you want to see Felicity, remember? Could we see them together?" He pushed a stray lock of hair away from her cheek.

"No. It's better to get people on their own. They are freer with their opinions about each other."

"You're really good at this," he said, a smile lighting his eyes.

"What?"

"Crime solving. Did you say there was a murder in Paris while you were there?"

Dodo nodded.

"Tell me about it."

For the next half an hour, she filled him in on her latest sleuthing caper.

His eyes became guarded with concern. "The murderer tried to kill you?"

Her spirits rose at the thought that he cared enough about her to worry. "I don't know if they would have gone through with it. Anyway, Renée arrived and saved the day."

"I say," he said tipping her chin with his finger. "Crime fighting is a dangerous game. You should be careful, Dodo."

Dodo felt a squeeze of gratitude that he had already taken on the role of her protector.

"I usually am. I either have Didi or Lizzie with me. I've learned my lesson."

"And now you have me."

"Yes. Now I have you." *At least while I try to figure out my feelings.*

A smile of contentment bubbled up from deep inside. With Charlie she was safe.

He placed a gentle kiss on her upturned lips. "Are you ready to go back? I think mother said dinner was at seven-thirty." He looked at his bulky, leather watch. "It's already six."

Dodo nodded.

He pulled her to her feet. "And we can use the telephone to arrange to meet Felicity and Portia. In spite of the danger, I can see why you like this stuff. Gets the blood going."

"Yes," she said with a laugh, "and it is so gratifying. It's like being able to mend a beautiful, smashed vase to perfection. Justice is seriously satisfying."

Charlie pressed another kiss to her mouth and then leaned his forehead against hers.

She sighed.
I could get used to this.

***

When they arrived back at Chadwick Hall, Charlie telephoned Felicity who invited him to her home for tea the next day, and Dodo arranged to meet Portia for supper the following evening.

After a swift, lavender-scented bath, Dodo dressed in a favorite cocktail gown. It was an ivory taffeta, with a deep V-neck, encrusted with bronze crystals. Exotic peacock feather patterns were hand-sewn around the hips, and rows and rows of bronze tassels dripped down to the ankles. It was all pulled together with a similarly encrusted bandeau that complemented her dark locks. Dangly earrings completed the look.

"Wow!" Charlie was waiting for her on the landing outside her door, leaning lazily against the doorframe of the room opposite.

"Hello lovely," he murmured as he kissed her. "You look amazing!" In spite of her reservations, she was pleased with the way Charlie had slid from friend to inamorato so seamlessly. And who didn't enjoy compliments?

He lifted his elbow. "Ready?"

Slipping her arm through his, they descended the stairs. She was an independent woman and proud of it, but she would be lying if she didn't admit that having someone care complete a part of her that had been missing.

They entered the drawing room where Charlie's parents were already enjoying an aperitif. It was a very traditional room, with dark, damask wallpaper, subdued sconce lighting, and thick Persian rugs.

"Darlings," cried Charlie's mother, Charlotte Chadwick. Whereas her own mother fought aging at every turn, Charlie's mother had gracefully surrendered.

Dodo noticed his mother take in their clasped hands and jerk her eyes up to study her son's face as she kissed them both. Her lips curled in a grin she could barely conceal. "It is so lovely to have you both here."

Mrs. Chadwick then sat in a chair across from them, ill-disguised curiosity evident on her face. Dodo had been a guest in this house many times but not as a girlfriend.

"How dreadful to hear about the murder yesterday." She was still staring at their intertwined arms.

Everyone had been in bed when they returned the evening before, and no one had appeared at breakfast so there had been no chance to discuss the murder before. Or address the change in their relationship status.

"Yes," replied Charlie, "and did you know it was someone who was a guest with us in the Guthrie's box?"

"No!" cried his mother. Her active eyes flitted from one face to the other. "Did you hear that, Crispin? They knew the man who was murdered!" Charlie's father was fixing them cocktails at an ornate, oak sideboard.

"I wouldn't say we knew him, Mother. He was just one of the other guests. He was new to his title and the Guthries were helping them along. He'd been an accountant or something before."

"How perfectly ghastly! I mean his being murdered—not that he was an accountant. Did it spoil your day?"

Charlie squeezed Dodo's hand; his mother's eyes lit up. "Yes, it did rather but we were having a lovely time before that." He looked at Dodo with affection.

Crispin Chadwick came over and handed them both a glass.

"I wanted to thank you for letting us use your royal passes," interjected Dodo. "It really was terribly thrilling to meet the King and Queen."

"Think nothing of it," said Charlie's mother. "Crispin couldn't make it, could you darling? And I didn't want to go alone. We actually get to see their Royal Highnesses quite often what with one thing and another." She knocked back the rest of her cocktail.

"Dinner is served," announced the butler who had appeared without a sound.

Charlie stood and gently led Dodo into the dining room across the hall. Mrs. Chadwick's cheeks ballooned with pride, and Dodo thought the woman might explode with joy at any moment.

If this doesn't work out, his mother is going to be seriously disappointed

Since it was just the four of them, they sat at one end of the large table and Mrs. Chadwick instructed the butler to seat Dodo next to Charlie. His mother was breaking all the rules.

The first dish was a clear soup that was a little too salty for Dodo's taste followed by rainbow trout, which was grilled to perfection. As they all enjoyed the meal the peal of the telephone could be heard.

A few minutes later the butler re-appeared.

"Excuse me, sir, but there is a Chief Inspector Blood on the telephone for Lady Dorothea."

Everyone turned to Dodo who was just raising a forkful of deliciousness into her mouth. At the mention of the chief inspector, her stomach dropped. With raised brows she replaced the fork and excused herself.

What on earth could he want?

"Hello, this is Lady Dorothea speaking." Her heart was ricocheting with nerves.

"M'lady." His voice was strained and brusque. "There has been another murder."

Chapter 9

Dodo collapsed to the chair in disbelief.

"Who?" A pit opened up in her stomach and she felt slightly dizzy.

"Lady…I mean, Mrs. Barchester."

"What? I had just been considering her as a suspect." Dodo considered how uncharitably she had looked on the woman's posture and dress and felt a stab of remorse.

"How was it done, Chief Inspector?"

"Poison. Looks like she had someone for tea, and they slipped it in her cup. They wore gloves as there are no useful fingerprints. Same with the knife, by the way, but in that case, there are too many fingerprints. Everyone seemed to use that knife."

Dodo thought again of people using the carving knife to slice the beef *after* it had been used to kill Lord Barchester, the blood of the victim and the meat juices combining. Her stomach lurched.

Fiendish.

"If I may ask, what led you to feel she was a good suspect?" asked the chief inspector.

Dodo quickly wiped her mouth with the back of her hand. "I thought she might have lied about why she left to find her husband. I thought it more probable that she *did* notice Felicity leave around the same time as him and followed them."

"Why?"

"Oh, I forgot to tell you. We visited the Carrington-Blythe's today and they were quite verbose." She filled in the chief inspector on the connection between Felicity and Lord Barchester.

"Ah, that does throw a different light on the matter. Lord Barchester and Felicity Snodgrass. Not a relationship I could have guessed at."

In spite of her queasiness and shock, she noticed that he was speaking to her as an equal. "Indeed! However, she was vulnerable and if he showed her a little sympathy…" She let the idea dangle.

"I suppose." By his tone she could imagine his face full of disgust.

"Anyway, I was just beginning to lean the other way, about Mrs. Barchester I mean. Barty Carrington-Blythe proposed a theory—in jest—casting her as the murderer, but his narrative included the idea that the murderer slipped the knife back into her handbag. It sparked a memory of finding Mrs. Barchester leaning over her husband's body. She was *not* carrying a bag."

"And her murder seems to corroborate your latest opinion of her."

The only thing Lady Barchester now seemed guilty of was trying too hard to be accepted. "It does rather." She leaned her head against the wall of the glass cabinet. A small silence descended as they were each lost in their own thoughts.

"We interviewed the next Lord Barchester," began the chief inspector, changing the subject. "Thoroughly awful chap who I'd be happy to pin the murder—both murders—on. However, he has a cast-iron alibi."

"Oh?"

"He was in the hospital having his arm set in a cast. His horse threw him, and he landed badly."

"That is a rather compelling alibi, I have to admit. Why didn't you like him?" Her stomach was beginning to settle.

"Full of his own importance and convinced that the title should have been his all along. No sympathy for his cousin whatsoever. He has a superiority complex. No wonder the blasted horse threw him off!"

The chief inspector chuckled but then seemed to realize that it was inappropriate under the circumstances.

"Did you learn anything else?" he asked.

"Not yet. We've set up a meeting with Felicity to ask her why she was upset at the dinner party with the hope that she'll tell us what happened with Lord Barchester, and another with Portia."

She put the earpiece to her other ear.

"Do you remember asking the colonel where he served in the military? Well, I forgot what he said but Charlie says someone—he thinks it was Portia—told them in passing that Lord Barchester served in the Far East. It jogged my memory. I think that's where the colonel served too. I want to see if Portia knows any more. Perhaps Lord Barchester's death is connected to something in his past?"

"Could be. I'm glad you are interviewing the girls. That will be most helpful. I need to put my resources into the new murder as well as the old. We are stretched pretty thin. Mrs. Barchester had already moved back into their old home since they hadn't sold it yet, and that is where she was murdered. My constables are in the process of questioning the neighbors, the maid, and the cook. Unfortunately, it was their day off. Wednesday. Most domestic servants have Wednesday afternoons off. Plus, the house is a thatched cottage in the country on several acres of land. The nearest neighbor is at least a quarter of a mile away so I don't hold out much hope, but procedure must be followed."

"I still can't believe it," Dodo said, her mind spinning as she considered that someone had stalked the poor widow.

"I admit I did not see this coming. I feel a little…responsible."

She rushed to his defense. "Come, come Chief Inspector. How could you have known?" She gripped the telephone tightly. "The person responsible is the murderer."

"I suppose so. Good evening, Lady Dorothea." The usual authoritative assurance was missing in his voice, betraying how much the second murder was weighing on his conscience. For the first time in their acquaintance, she pitied him.

"Good evening, Chief Inspector."

She replaced the earpiece slowly and sat, pondering. She understood the chief inspector's feelings of responsibility, as the first shoots of guilt started to spring up, accusing her of failing the poor woman. But she had never considered that Mrs. Barchester would be in danger. The murderer had acted quickly which meant they felt that the former Lady Barchester remained a threat. She experienced a rush of sympathy for the homely woman who had been thrust into a society that did not readily accept her, only to lose her husband and then her own life.

When Dodo returned to the dining room, all three faces looked at her with nervous anticipation.

Not one to sugar coat things, she declared, "Lady Barchester has been murdered."

Charlie and his parents gasped.

"I know. It's terrible. I'm still in shock." She gripped the back of the chair, her stomach cramping. "Lady Barchester did not deserve this."

Charlie grabbed for her hand and squeezed as she sat. The warmth and tenderness of his touch was comforting. Even if she did not yet consider him her sweetheart he was, and always had been, a marvelous friend.

"Did the chief inspector tell you how?" Charlie's mother asked.

"She was poisoned. Someone came to tea and slipped it in her cup—well, that's their working theory." Dodo looked at her plate. The trout no longer held any appeal. She pushed it far from her.

Charlie placed his arm gently across her shoulder. The affectionate act caused her eyes to prickle and she had a sudden urge to cry. Instead, she shook her head and swallowed hard.

"The chief inspector said he felt a strange responsibility. I told him that was nonsense, but I feel it too," she admitted.

"Why on earth would you?" asked Charlie.

"If I had discovered the murderer already, I could have prevented this."

Charlie's father, an older version of his son, frowned. "Isn't that the responsibility of Scotland Yard?"

"Father is right, Dodo," said Charlie. "You are merely assisting the police with their inquiries. This is *not* your fault."

***

Felicity lived in a spacious Victorian apartment in the middle of Windsor. It had high ceilings, large French windows, original Impressionist artwork, and ultra-modern furniture. In Dodo's opinion, it needed a professional touch.

Felicity had started on seeing both of them at her door, as Charlie had purposely not mentioned that Dodo would be with him, but graciously showed the two of them in, calling the maid for another cup and saucer. On the way, Dodo had suggested that Charlie should take the lead in the conversation, giving him ideas of some questions.

"I was surprised to get your call," she said, directing her words to Charlie with a coquettish smile. She had obviously taken great care with her hair and make-up.

"Things got cut short at Ascot by the murder. We felt it was left kind of unfinished," he explained, indicating Dodo with his hand.

Felicity bestowed a dirty glare Dodo's way. If looks could kill she'd be dead.

She looked back at Charlie. "I've been having trouble sleeping actually," she confessed.

"Really?" Charlie slid forward in the Nordic style chair.

"Yes. I knew him a little bit. Lord Barchester. Makes all the difference when you know the person rather than reading about some stranger in the paper." She seemed to remember her scar and pulled her hair forward to screen it.

"I agree." Dodo recognized Charlie's soft expression. He was pulling out all the stops. Perhaps she should have let him come alone.

"I met him at a dinner party, like I said the day at the races, but umm…I actually had a little more interaction with him than I told the police." She dropped her gaze and poured the tea, using a delicate silver tea strainer.

"What do you mean?" Charlie pretended ignorance.

If Charlie leans forward anymore, he's going to fall off the chair entirely.

Felicity handed them each a cup and offered some tiny cakes without actually looking at Dodo once.

"I'm sure you have wondered about my scar…" Subconsciously her fingers found the ugly mark and traced along it.

They both remained diplomatically quiet.

"A horse kicked me," she began. "I was lucky not to have been hurt more, they say. It was an accident. Alexander was on a horse that got spooked and I was standing too close. These things happen." She had taken the words and fashioned them into a cupid's arrow that she shot straight at Charlie's sympathies. It was as if Dodo wasn't even there. She could feel indignation rising.

"Alex has dealt with a lot of guilt about it." Felicity locked eyes with Charlie. "Actually, I don't think we would still be together if it hadn't happened. He feels responsible—as if he owes me a debt. It's misguided."

Gone was the angsty woman from the day of the races. This was a new and improved Felicity. "I was having a bad night at the dinner party," she continued, speaking only to Charlie. "People were talking about me, whispering behind their hands, and I was struggling. No one was on the patio and I went out to try to pull myself together, but I broke down." She looked down at her feet, fingering the scar.

"While I was there, someone came out and heard me crying. He was so sweet and crouched down by me, not asking any questions, just soothing me. Then he took my hand and stroked it, a kindness that helped me get my breathing under control. I didn't even realize that he had risen and sat on the bench until he put his arm around me. One thing led to another and…he kissed me." She raised her head, tears brimming in her eyes. "It was sweet and tender but almost immediately he pulled back. He made an excuse and went back inside. I followed.

"His wife was there, waiting and glared at me as I entered the room from the patio. I think she knew. I hadn't even known he was married."

Dodo was dying to ask her a million questions but was pretty sure Felicity would clam up if she entered the conversation. She kept her curiosity in check.

"You must have been so surprised to see him at Ascot," said Charlie.

"I was! I had no idea they had been invited. Lady Barchester looked daggers at me, and I kept well out of her way. But Lord Barchester took the occasion to apologize for his behavior and hoped I would forgive him. He was a sweet man. I'm sad he's dead."

"Did you slip him a note? Try to set up a meeting?" Charlie asked.

"No!" Felicity's response was adamant. "It wasn't like that. It was just a moment of weakness. Nothing more." Her head snapped up. "Why would you think that?"

"I thought I saw you two leave the box around the same time."

"That was a coincidence. He didn't even see me. I went to the ladies' and he went the other way." She batted her eyelashes and Dodo had to refrain from rolling her eyes.

"It feels so much better to get that off my chest," Felicity sighed.

"What about Alexander? Did he know about the kiss?" asked Charlie.

"Heavens no! He wasn't at the dinner party." She rearranged the dainty china plates that held the cakes. "He's actually a little intense for me, if I'm honest. It irritates me, all this bravado about overthrowing the monarchy and such. I think I'm going to break things off with him soon. Very soon." She pinned Charlie with a 'come-hither' look. Dodo's dislike of her was growing by the minute.

"So, you don't sympathize with his revolutionary leanings?" asked Charlie.

Felicity chuckled. "I'm not sure he does himself. It's pretty safe to hold such views when the possibility of getting your hands dirty is remote, and he has a healthy allowance from his family's wealth. He's all talk."

Charlie thanked her for the tea and made to leave.

"Going so soon?" she crooned.

"Ah…yes. We have lots of things on our plate today."

Felicity gave Dodo the once over and asked, "Do you know if the police have any suspects?" Charlie and Dodo caught each other's eye. The police seemed to have gone to great pains to keep the second murder out of the papers.

"No," said Charlie. "We're in the dark."

"If I had to guess, I would think it was his wife. There was obviously something boiling under the surface," said Felicity.

"Perhaps," replied Charlie. "Thanks again."

Dodo could barely contain herself until they were back on the street before declaring, "Great Scott! If I hadn't been there, she would have been all over you!"

"I don't know what you mean," said Charlie, while pulling her close.

Dodo slapped his arm with her white, kid gloves.

"Are you jealous, Lady Dorothea?" He fastened her with his piercing blue gaze.

Was she?

"As much as that charade made me uncomfortable, I think we can cross her off the list," she conceded.

"Really? What makes you so sure? She just confessed to having a moment with his lordship." His left eye was squinted with skepticism.

Dodo placed her hands on his broad shoulders. "Because she obviously doesn't know that Mrs. Barchester has been murdered."

Chapter 10

Dodo and Charlie met Portia at an exclusive restaurant in Cobham, near her family's home in Surrey. Pains had been taken to make the outside of the building look older than it was with decorative plaster. Greek columns lining the patio entrance lent a pleasing Italian aura. A soft light welcomed them as they entered, the product of dim electric lights around the soffit and candles on each table. The inner walls were lined with greenery and plaster statues of women in togas holding water jugs on their shoulders. A satisfying garlicky aroma wafted on the air.

Dodo's stomach rumbled in pleasant anticipation.

As they entered hand in hand, Portia waved at them. She had traded the polka dots for a garish floral print. Beaming with pleasurable anticipation, she beckoned them over. Portia was one of those enviable people brimming over with a natural enthusiasm for life.

"I was so thrilled to get your invitation," she gushed.

"Yes, we felt like things were left unfinished on race day. Incomplete," said Dodo.

"I know what you mean. After I left, I felt very strange. Slept in fits and starts with horrible nightmares." She put her palm to her forehead, knocking a glittery head bandeau slightly askew. Dodo tried not to let the crookedness bother her.

The waiter came over and they all took a moment to look at the menu. Portia was a regular and gave them a running commentary on the different dishes.

As the waiter withdrew, Portia's eyes lit up with eager curiosity. "So, have you heard anything new?"

The chief inspector had still not given Dodo authority to disclose the fact that there had been a second murder, and the papers were conspicuously quiet on the subject. However, Dodo felt that if they offered Portia an exclusive piece of information, she might open up to them.

"We *did* learn that the murder weapon was the carving knife for the roast beef." She and Charlie had discussed which piece of the puzzle to disclose, gauging that Portia was of a strong constitution.

Portia reared back, hand to her mouth. "Oh, my word! The carving knife? I used it while the police were questioning people!" Her face turned a dangerous shade of green. Closing her eyes, she gulped while clutching her stomach. Dodo and Charlie exchanged a worried look.

Wrong opener!

"I'm so sorry. I had no idea." Dodo tried to backtrack.

Portia suddenly jumped up. "I'll be right back."

They watched helplessly as she weaved unsteadily among the tables to the ladies' bathroom.

Charlie's face creased into an endearing frown. "Oops."

"Bad miscalculation," Dodo said, grimacing. "I may have just ruined things. What if she doesn't some back and sneaks off home? I was sure she was the type of girl who could handle it."

Charlie placed a comforting hand on her shoulder. "You couldn't have known she had used the knife *after* the murder. Look how it affected us and we didn't even use the knife? We took a gamble, and it didn't pay off. These things happen. Let's wait for a bit."

The waiter brought their starters, but neither one had the appetite for it and the plates lay untouched on the table while they waited in awkward silence to see how things would unfold. Charlie started tapping the table-top with his fork and Dodo fiddled with her bracelet.

After ten full minutes had passed, Dodo was about to send out a search party when Portia could be seen threading her way back to them. Damp little ringlets clung to the sides of her ample face. The bandeau was gone but her color was back to normal.

She sat down heavily with her hand to her chest. "Woah, that caught me right between the eyes. Took a while to get a grip on myself. I'm fine now," she assured them. She glanced down at her food but pushed the plate away and instead took a great gulp of wine.

"Please accept my apologies," said Dodo.

"Oh, it's not your fault. I should have shown more respect for the dead at the time and stopped eating. I'm a bit of a nervous eater, truth be told." She picked up the napkin and wiped her cheeks, staring at the white tablecloth as if it held all the answers.

"And it's not as though you knew him," remarked Dodo.

"We didn't know him either," said Charlie. "But Felicity did."

"Yes, I saw them talking." Portia looked up and pushed a damp curl behind one ear.

"Did you?" asked Dodo. "What were their expressions like? Could you tell if it was small talk or was it something more"—Dodo narrowed her eyes— "intimate?"

"Do you know something?" Interest stole over Portia's face as she replaced the napkin and leaned forward.

"We do," said Dodo. "But I'd like your take on it before we muddy the waters. What do you remember?"

"Hmm." Portia's mouth twisted as she examined the recesses of her memory. "Felicity was going to get some food when Lord Barchester intercepted her and I could immediately tell that she recognized him. He bent his head to her and spoke quietly with a serious expression. I remember wondering what they could be talking about. Then I saw Felicity lock eyes with Lady Barchester while he was talking. The smile dropped from Felicity's face like a rock in a pond and she came back to our table." Portia took another swig of wine.

Dodo laced her fingers, resting her chin on them and looked at Charlie. This confirmed Felicity's account of events.

"Now, tell me what you know!" Portia demanded. Clearly, she was not above a little common gossip. Perhaps if Portia knew the truth about Felicity and Lord Barchester she would view all the events she witnessed that day through a different prism and remember something else important.

Dodo glanced around to make sure no one was listening. "Well…" said Dodo, stringing out the word. "Lord Barchester and Felicity met at a dinner party a few months before … and he kissed her."

"Kissed her? What? An old fellow like *that*, kiss Felicity?" Disbelief hung from her features like rain on an umbrella.

Dodo rested her cheek on her fist. "It's true. We heard it from Felicity herself. It would explain the nasty look his wife gave her."

Portia was still shaking her head, evidently incredulous.

"Remember the awful gash on her face?" asked Charlie.

Portia's eyes grew round.

"It was still fresh when she attended the party," continued Dodo, "and people were babbling about it behind her back. Felicity was very upset and had gone out to the patio to cry in private. Lord Barchester found her and offered a little sympathy."

"Well, I never!" Portia raised her hands knocking over her glass and spilling red wine all over the white cloth. Charlie grabbed all the napkins and began blotting up the mess. "Oh, I'm so clumsy!" Portia exclaimed. "Here, let me do it." She took the soaking napkins from Charlie and dabbed at the bloodlike stain.

"I'm just so surprised," she continued as she wiped. "But that would certainly explain the glower from Lady Barchester?"

"Yes, he and his wife had a rather public disagreement after that. Perhaps Lord Barchester had a penchant for younger ladies?" Dodo made a mental note to mention this idea to the chief inspector when they next spoke.

"Did it look as though they were making plans to meet when you saw them speaking?" asked Charlie.

Abandoning the stain, she paused, crinkling her nose as she thought. "I don't think so. Felicity looked rather awkward actually, as though she was a bit embarrassed. Now I know why! I bet she never thought she would see him again." Portia chewed her lip.

"And yet, Felicity left the box right after him." Dodo introduced the fact that could mean that Felicity was lying about where she went.

"That's true," agreed Portia, "but Felicity and Lord Barchester?" She shook her head with disdain. "Besides, she was with Alexander. And why would she kill Lord Barchester if she liked him? Anyway, she returned within five minutes. Would that have been enough time?" Questions were pouring out of her like water from a canal lock.

"You are sure she came back that soon?" asked Dodo, her fingers gripping the fork. "How do you know?"

"Because Alexander was checking his watch when she came back. He kept her on a tight leash if you ask me."

Dodo slumped in her chair. "That would *not* have given her time," Dodo conceded. Even though she had concluded herself that Felicity was not the culprit, the way she had brazenly flirted with Charlie the day before had left her with a great dislike for the girl.

Charlie pounced on the comment about Alexander. "What did you think of their relationship? Felicity and Alexander? Did you think they seemed fond of each other?"

Portia's lips puckered. "Now that you mention it, no. She seemed irritated by his boorish manner. He kept challenging people on what they said all the time. I didn't take to him at all. It was supposed to be a pleasant, relaxing day."

Charlie put his knife and fork down. "Would it surprise you to learn that Alexander was the cause of her injury?"

"Really? Did he hit her?" Dodo thought it telling that everyone jumped to that conclusion. "Although he was constantly arguing his position, I got the impression that he was all bark."

Portia was a pretty astute judge of character.

"No," explained Dodo. "He was on a horse that got startled and it bucked, clipping Felicity on the cheek."

Portia picked up a forkful of stuffed mushrooms and then thought better of it. "Ah." She waved the fork around. "He feels guilty. That explains it. He's only still with her because he feels responsible."

"Spot on!" said Charlie. "Felicity told us the same thing herself."

"Which actually fuels the case for a secret rendezvous between her and his Lordship, does it not?" added Dodo.

Portia was shaking her head. "No. No. Felicity wasn't feeling vulnerable the day of the race. Angry at Alexander—yes. Irritated—yes. But not sad or depressed. No, in the cold light of day, I bet she saw Lord Barchester for what he was, just a homely, middle-aged man whose wife was in the room." She shuddered.

The waiter came back to collect their plates and started when he saw the state of the tablecloth and that no food had been touched.

His forehead puckered. "Was the food not to your liking?"

"It was fine," Portia assured him. "We just had some bad news that stole our appetites briefly. We're ready for the next course now."

The waiter grabbed the plates and waddled off like an angry goose.

Dodo leaned forward. "But the police found a note on Lord Barchester setting up a meeting for four o' clock under the stands."

Portia's eyes popped. "And they think it was from Felicity?"

"That is one theory. She denied it." Dodo smoothed the wet cloth. "But someone had gone to great lengths to disguise their handwriting. It looked as though it was written by a right-hander with the left hand."

"And Lord Barchester must have assumed it was from Felicity." Portia had good instincts.

She slapped the table. "Then it was from his wife!"

"That is the logical conclusion, but the police have infallible evidence that it was not her," stated Dodo.

Portia shifted in her chair. "Alibi's can be fabricated, surely."

"This one is solid," Charlie confirmed.

Portia raised a brow.

"The chief inspector did not give me authority to disclose how he knows, but I expect you will find out soon enough."

Portia's nose wrinkled again. "You know the inspector?"

"Chief Inspector Blood and I met at another incident," Dodo explained. "I played a small part in discovering the culprit."

"Actually," interrupted Charlie, "she solved the whole thing."

"Did you?" Portia's chin dropped and her mouth formed an 'o'. "So that's why he let you listen in on our interviews?"

Dodo puckered her lips in an attempt to look humble "Yes."

Dodo was relieved when the waiter returned, breaking the conversation and giving her a natural pause in which to redirect the conversation.

"Do I remember you saying that you saw the colonel shaking his head when Lord Barchester spoke to him? You didn't happen to hear what they were talking about, did you?"

Portia's face pinched as she considered.

"Could it have been about the Far East?" Charlie prompted.

"Burma? Is that the Far East?" Portia's bottom lip pulled down. "I'm abysmal at geography."

"It is," Dodo confirmed. Portia may have learned more from her observations than even Portia realized. Dodo would have to formulate her questions carefully. "So, they were talking about Burma?"

"I wasn't really paying attention, but I did hear that country mentioned and then the colonel shook his head."

"Perhaps Lord Barchester was asking the colonel if he was ever stationed there?" Dodo prodded.

"Possibly." Portia did not look convinced.

Now that some time had passed, everyone tucked into their food. Dodo wrapped her fork in spaghetti as her mind tried to wrap itself around the things she had learned over the last two days. Details danced around like sprites and she tried to rein them in. She wished she had her notebook.

The murder could not be about the title since the cousin had an alibi and there would be no need to kill his wife. And as much as she might dislike Felicity, she really did not seem to have either a motive or opportunity. She felt no farther along than when they had arrived.

Charlie, polite as ever, was neatly cutting his roast beef and chatting companionably with Portia who was attacking her crab pasta with gusto.

Coming out of her reverie, Dodo joined the conversation again. "How are things with Roger?"

Portia's cheeks rose and a pink flush blossomed. "He's taking me out to the coast next week. I'm so excited. Usually chaps go for the likes of you or Felicity. Can't believe my luck!"

Dodo was beginning to think Roger might be the lucky one.

***

Driving back to the Chadwick estate, Charlie shifted in his seat.

"I'm hoping to get a new one soon."

"Car?" Dodo asked.

"Yes, I'm sure you're used to traveling in much more style."

"It doesn't bother me at all," she said, but that was not entirely true. She loved the sleek lines of her family Bentley, but she had no intention of hurting Charlie's feelings. She knew that he had overcome his gambling addiction, and there had been debts to be paid. She respected him for that.

The night sky danced with the light of a thousand stars as they drove. "Did you hear anything tonight that got your brilliant brain turning?" Charlie asked as he reached for her hand across the gear shift. She was not in the least upset about this.

"Actually, I did. The more I consider it the more I think how creepy it was that Lord Barchester would kiss someone so much younger than he, especially when they had only just met. If he had a proclivity for that kind of behavior, perhaps he made someone angry?"

If someone took their revenge, maybe Lady Barchester was an unwitting witness.

An owl swooped across the road in front of them.

"How would we find that out?" asked Charlie, threading his fingers through hers.

"He had only been an earl for a short while. Let's find out if he dallied with the young ladies at his accounting job."

The lateness of the hour meant that the roads were free of traffic as the old Ford wound its way along the dark country roads.

"Anything else rattling around in that beautiful head of yours?" He lifted their hands and softly kissed her knuckles. She sighed with contentment. She could definitely do worse.

"I think it is a matter of interest that Lord Barchester talked to the colonel about Burma. The Far East is a big place, and Burma's not a popular watering hole, after all. I think we should dig into Lord Barchester's military career a bit, see what we uncover."

"You don't suspect the colonel surely?" Charlie briefly took his eyes from the road.

"I suspect everyone until proven innocent."

Charlie whistled. "I kind of like this side of you. Strong and determined."

"Even though I suspected you once?" she ventured, laying her cards on the table.

"Really? At Farrington Hall with the maid?" He removed his hand from the steering wheel making the little car weave and put it to his chest in a show of mock horror.

She shot him a coy smile. "Like I said, I suspect everyone."

"Well, I *was* guilty," he said, returning his eyes to the road and his hand to the wheel.

Dodo turned her head sharply to look at him.

"Of being spitting jealous of your relationship with Julian."

Dodo threw back her head and laughed.

Chapter 11

"Well, hello," said the smooth voice of David Bellamy, an old friend of Dodo's who worked in the City in stocks and bonds. He had been a valuable asset in helping her with one of her other cases. She could imagine him sitting at his desk in his dark, blue suit, crisp, white shirt, his dirty blond hair falling over his left eye as it always did.

"Hello David." She was sitting in the Chadwick Hall telephone cabinet once again looking at the familiar oak paneled walls, tense with fidgety anticipation. If anyone could help her it would be David.

She and David were old friends and had last seen each other at his cousin's wedding where she had gone as his guest as 'payment' for his help. She couldn't imagine why he didn't have a girlfriend; he was friendly, wealthy, and successful.

They caught up on each other's lives for a while then David asked why she had really called.

"I'm in the middle of a little problem again," she said, knowing he was going to tease her.

"I know you. Your little problems are other people's nightmares. Who died this time?" His tone was tongue in cheek.

She gripped the ivory earpiece a little tighter. "Actually…did you read about Lord Barchester's murder at Ascot?"

"My dear girl! *That* is your little problem? What an exciting life you lead!"

She puckered her lips. "Murder just seems to find me." Flinging the pale organza scarf back around her neck, she continued, "Lord Barchester used to work in the City as plain Mr. Jeremy Barchester. Could you put out some feelers and see what you find?"

His merry laugh trilled down the line. "I need a little more to go on than that, Dodo. Come on, spill the beans. What do you suspect him of doing?"

Naturally, he would want the gossip. I'd better set some ground rules. "This is strictly confidential, you understand?"

"Of course. I'm silent as the grave."

Liar. A couple of drinks and your lips become very loose.

She sighed. "He kissed a girl young enough to be his daughter—a girl he had just met—at a dinner party. I'm interested to know if he made a habit of it."

"Scandal! I love it!"

"David…" she warned.

"I know, I know. Strictly confidential. Mum's the word."

"Thank you."

Wait for it.

"It will cost you," he retorted, as she had known he would. "I've got another bally cousin getting married."

"Of course I'll go with you… I'll just have to run it by my current beau." She wrinkled her nose waiting for the shoe to drop.

David's irreverent tone changed. "You're off the market?"

"David! I'm not a blasted cow up for auction."

"Didn't mean to offend, old thing. Who's the lucky chap?"

"Charlie Chadwick. I grew up with him. Things have recently progressed."

"Good for you. If it doesn't work out, you have my number." She could hear the grin spread across his mobile features down the phone line.

"Goodbye, David."

As she replaced the earpiece, she wondered about her statement that Charlie was her beau. It was the first time she had referred to him as such, even to herself. Was it true? Shouldn't she be seeing fireworks and experiencing heart palpitations? Her thoughts circled back to her mother. This was more of a slow burn type of relationship, like hers and Daddy's. Dodo just needed to give it time.

***

Dodo had concluded that it would be helpful to compare notes with Chief Inspector Blood in person. She and Charlie had arranged to go to Scotland Yard in the late afternoon and take advantage of some of the tourist sites while they were in town. Though she had grown up a mere forty-five-minute train ride from London, she still thrilled at the majesty of the historic buildings and verdant parks of the capital city.

Though the rain had run down the windows of the train on their journey, the sun had come out to greet them as they descended at Charing Cross and was now shining as though it had something to prove. She and Charlie were currently walking, arm in arm, down the Mall toward Buckingham Palace.

Lots of people were out on the pond in St James' park on paddle boats. Pigeons were abundant, scavenging for crumbs left by visitors, and British flags flapped everywhere.

"This is one of my very favorite places." Dodo shaded her eyes with her hand as they looked down the long road toward the palace. "It has such ambience."

"I've only been here a few times," Charlie admitted, "but I do see the appeal." When she checked his expression, he was looking at her, not the famous street.

They wandered in the direction of the palace, enjoying the warm, summer sunshine. "Do you know why it's called The Mall?" Dodo asked.

"Enlighten me." Charlie's lips hitched up a little on the right. She felt a slight catch in her chest.

"It started life as a field for playing the game 'pall-mall'—a sort of pre-cursor to croquet."

"You are a wealth of information," he said, grabbing her by the waist and drawing her close.

Very close.

So close she could feel his heartbeat through her dress and his warm breath gently fanning her face.

Losing herself in the hazy details of his blue eyes she witnessed a variety of emotions, ending in desire, vibrating through them. His intensity swallowed up her doubts.

His chocolate brown waves had been blown awry by the breeze, and he looked deliciously casual.

Attractive.

His expression lost its mirth.

"Dodo…" He whispered her name as though it physically hurt.

His hand slipped around her neck with the softness of a silk ribbon and he drew her to him. She surrendered to the moment, putting up no resistance. His expert kiss did not push or demand; it was tender and sweet. Drawing the kiss out, then pressing his forehead to hers, his breath was ragged.

"Dodo, I really like you."

A shower of responses flooded her…including guilt. Much as she had savored the soft kiss, it still sparked no fire in her veins. Facing a moral dilemma, she batted the confusion away. She has resolved to give it more time, hadn't she? Perhaps such things as fireworks were only in fantasies? The stuff of fairy tales. There was no question that with Charlie she felt safe and protected. She would be a fool to spoil this.

She offered him a wistful smile. "I like you too."

He released her waist while maintaining his hold on her hand and clicked his heels, whooping out loud for everyone in the world to hear. His jubilation was infectious, and she felt contentment effervescing within her.

Turning to peer at her with those clear blue eyes again, his face shone like the sun breaking through the clouds after a storm.

I am happy.

They almost skipped all the way down to Buckingham Palace and then veered to the left along the cobble paths, past the homes of palace staff, flagging a taxi to take them to Westminster Bridge.

After snuggling in the back of the taxi, Charlie's mood was high when they arrived at the Thames, and he dragged her down the steps to the riverside as she giggled like a schoolgirl. He bought tickets for passage on a river cruiser and led her straight to the upper deck, right at the front. Standing behind her, his arms encircled her middle, and he tucked his chin against her neck.

It had been a long time since a man had treated her this way and she melted into him, breathing in the river breeze and watching the pigeons swoop and dip.

"I could stay like this all day," he breathed, his lips brushing her neck as he spoke.

"Me too." And she realized it was true.

Are love and happiness the same thing?

A fisherman on the river looked up, a worn rain cap shading his eyes. Seeing them on the boat he tipped his chin, lifting his pole in recognition of the young lovers. Dodo nodded back. Passing under a bridge, tourists waved, and she felt a lightness float over her. The wind gusted, picking up her ebony hair and slapping it against her cheeks. She flung her head back against Charlie's shoulder, abandoning herself to the precious moment.

When the vessel docked at the Tower, they descended and walked around the wide cobble paths admiring the immense, square castle with its green moat.

A street vendor was roasting almonds nearby in a steel cauldron. "Would you like some?" asked Charlie.

Dodo nodded. "Ooh, yes!"

Together they shared a brown paper bag, their fingers fighting for the treasures inside. Charlie lifted one up and brought it to her lips. "For you m'lady."

Somewhere a clock struck three.

"Boo. We should go," she said. "Our appointment is in half an hour." She was truly sorry that their romantic escape was over, heartened that with careful watering this relationship might blossom into something bigger.

Charlie flagged down a cab and they wound their way through the busy streets of London to Scotland Yard.

On arrival they were directed to the second floor and knocked on a battered, black door that was in need of some attention. Dodo could smell lemon polish mixed with floor cleaner.

"Come in."

Dodo felt a jolt as the chief inspector's gruff voice came through the door.

Charlie turned the handle and she followed behind. The chief inspector had his head down, writing furiously. "I'll be with you in a moment."

Two moth-eaten chairs faced his desk and they sat. Charlie reached for her hand as he had done all day. Suddenly his hand felt like a holly bush.

"Now then." The chief inspector finally lifted his head. "Oh, is it three-thirty already?" His eyes came to rest on their hands and Dodo felt hot.

"I apologize," he said, hauling his gaze back up, brushing his hand across the tip of his nose. "I lost track of the time." He placed his pen carefully on the desk and clasped his hands in front of him. "What can you tell me?"

Dodo informed the chief inspector of the things they had discovered since they spoke on the phone and about her inquiries in the City. As she spoke, she withdrew her hand from Charlie's under the guise of checking that her hair was in place.

The chief inspector fiddled with a paperclip. "On my end, I can confirm that the carving knife was definitely the murder weapon."

"You should have seen Portia's reaction when we told her that was probably the weapon." Charlie was leaning forward, relaxed, his forearms on his thighs. He appeared blind to Dodo's nervous tension. "She had to run to the ladies'."

A glint shone in the chief inspector's coppery eyes. "It is rather ghoulish."

"But Portia used the knife to cut herself some beef *after* the murder," explained Charlie.

"Ah," remarked the chief inspector.

Dodo forced herself to smile. She thought her face might crack.

"After extensive questioning I can also confirm that no one saw anything at the Barchester's place," Chief Inspector Blood continued. "The killer must have arrived on foot, unannounced, after waiting for the maids to leave." He looked everywhere but directly at Dodo. "So that is a dead end."

"What poison do they think was used?" She forced herself to speak, though her heart was ricocheting around in her ribcage.

"Arsenic. Available in any corner store for dealing with rats. That's a dead end too."

The chief inspector shuffled some papers and a small business card fell to the floor. Dodo reached down to pick it up and as she handed it back her fingers brushed the chief inspector's.

Lightning bolted up her arm and she locked eyes with him. He quickly looked away.

Dodo turned to check that Charlie hadn't noticed the exchange, but his jaw was tense, his eyes haunted.

Drat!

She fidgeted in her seat and swallowed hard

The chief inspector pulled down his cuffs.

"We've checked into Alexander," he continued as the air in the room grew thick. "He has already caught the attention of the Dean at his college, both because he is behind in his work and due to his political leanings. However, we can find no connection between him and Lord Barchester. He is a thoroughly obnoxious young man, but my gut tells me it's not him."

"Could he have been jealous if he thought there was something between Lord Barchester and Felicity?" Dodo's voice was tight and unnatural sounding even to her own ears. Coming here with Charlie had been a bad idea.

What was I thinking?

"Do you really think he's that fond of her?" The chief inspector tilted his head and Dodo felt her stomach clench.

"No. Felicity made it sound like she was going to break it off."

Charlie was unnaturally quiet. She desperately cast around for another question.

"What about Alistair and the barmaid?"

"His alibi is solid. She confirms he was with her at the time of the murder. In fact, she won some money on one of the races."

An awkward silence pervaded the space and Dodo eyed the window.

"Have you spoken to the Guthries by any chance?" The chief inspector glanced at Charlie who was looking at the floor.

"Do you want us to?" she said.

"This second murder is using a lot of my resources, and the people upstairs are breathing down my neck to close the case. The fact that the King and Queen were in the area, as the papers keep pointing out, has them very nervous. The Guthries are on my list, but I am seeing the colonel and his wife tomorrow." He motioned to Charlie. "Since you know them, I thought it would save some time."

"Of course." Charlie's voice was flat.

A million bats flapping in her brain could not have felt worse than the awkwardness that was thick in the room and Dodo had to suppress the instinct to flee. "Are you looking into Lord Barchester's military service? That is the kind of thing *we* just don't have the contacts for." Her shoulders were as stiff as an iron rod.

What is happening? How could such a perfect day take such a bad turn?

"Yes, I've got people searching his background and Lady Barchester's."

"And we still don't know who the note was from?"

"No. I'm having it analyzed but it looks like they went to great lengths to disguise their writing."

The office had become impossibly stuffy and Dodo could stand it no longer. "Right-o then," she said, jumping up. "We'll meet with the Guthries and get back to you." She turned, ready to bolt for the door.

The chief inspector stood and put out his arm to shake hands with Charlie who responded with a limp hand. Then he moved in Dodo's direction. A sudden reluctance to make contact with him grabbed her but she forced her hand up. As they touched, she felt the spark of heat again but kept her eyes firmly on the desk.

"Thanks for coming in," the chief inspector said as he saw them both to the door.

Descending the stairs under a cloud, Dodo took a huge breath of sooty, London air when they got outside.

"What was *that?*" Charlie's tone was sharp, his brow deeply creased.

"What?" she replied biting her bottom lip, a nervous hole growing in her stomach.

Charlie paced around on the sidewalk. "What? The inspector couldn't take his eyes off you."

It was time for some big-time deception.

She opened her eyes as wide as she could. "Whatever do you mean?"

Charlie ignored her protestation. "Is there something going on between the two of you?"

She forced out a bark of a laugh. "Do you know how ridiculous that sounds?" She grabbed Charlie's hand. "But jealousy looks good on you."

Charlie frowned, searching her face as she waited on tenterhooks. Then his angry expression collapsed, and his face softened.

"I'm an idiot."

The insecurity dropped from his features, and a smile quivered across his lips. Dodo experienced a sudden urge to kiss them.

Pulling his jacket collar tight to her, she planted a hard, long smooch, cabs and cars whizzing behind them. When they came up for air, Charlie was back to himself, the confident fellow who was friends with everyone. A laugh rumbled in his throat. "Sorry I doubted you. I'm not usually so insecure."

He seized her hand, his face now full of smiles, and hailed a cab to take them back to the train station. As he did so, Dodo looked up just in time to spot Chief Inspector Blood pulling back from the dirty window.

Chapter 12

Dodo tossed and turned in her bed at Chadwick Hall, her conscience howling, her mind racing with confusion. Her insides were a riot of mixed emotions. Try as she might she could not shut off her brain as it continually contrasted the two men.

Just when she felt like she had a handle on her feelings for Charlie, the chief inspector had confused her. *Why did he have the power to rattle her, so?* It was infuriating.

He was infuriating.

But that touch. The heat.

She had never felt such charged stirrings from being close to Charlie.

But it was absurd.

The chief inspector was too old, too grumpy, and most importantly, they were from different sides of the tracks. In fact, they were from different sides of the planet. The universe!

She didn't even *like* him.

Finally dropping into a fitful sleep, she awoke a few hours later in a foul mood, the sheets thrashed and threaded through her legs.

She punched her pillow to within an inch of its life in frustration. It was time to forget the agitation of yesterday and focus all her energies on Charlie.

Dear, loveable Charlie.

***

Dodo somehow managed to get dressed in a long, blue, bias-cut skirt and simple poplin blouse. She barely spoke to the maid. Then she dragged her weary body into breakfast to find Charlie full of morning sunshine.

"Hello, beautiful!"

Charlie is here and he is my social equal. Weighed down with fatigue, she lifted a smile as anemic as weak tea.

He lifted the lid of one silver warmer to reveal fluffy, yellow eggs. Lack of sleep and heavy food did not mix, and her stomach turned unpleasantly. Groaning, she shook her head. "I'll just take some toast and tea, thank you."

Charlie shrugged and rolled his shoulders.

"Alistair called last night while we were out," he began. "Wants me to telephone him this morning."

When Dodo had eaten, she felt her spirits improve. She followed Charlie to the telephone cabinet and they both squeezed into the tiny closet that was designed for just one person.

When the call was put through to Alistair, Charlie beckoned to Dodo who pressed her cheek close to his so that they could both hear what was being said.

"Alistair, it's Charlie."

"Charlie. Thanks for calling back. Look, I've been wrestling with a bit of a guilty conscience."

Me too!

Charlie's mouth pulled down and a crease appeared at the top of his nose. It was adorable.

"Guilty conscience?"

Dodo and Charlie stared at each other in disbelief.

"Yes, I saw something the day of the murder that I didn't tell the chief inspector."

Dodo arched a finely plucked eyebrow.

"Go on," said Charlie.

"I didn't say anything as I didn't want to get anyone in trouble, and I am absolutely positive they had nothing to do with the murder…but the remorse is eating me alive."

"You'll feel better once you tell someone, old chap," Charlie encouraged him.

There was a pause. Dodo gripped Charlie's arm wondering what on earth Alistair was going to say. But Alistair was clearly having second thoughts.

"I suppose I want your advice as to whether it's something I *should* tell Chief Inspector Blood."

"Of course." Charlie pursed his lips, brooding anticipation written all over his face, but he didn't push. Dodo was impressed. Impatience was threatening to swallow her whole. It was taking all her effort not to grab the phone and shout at Alistair to get on with it.

Finally, he continued, his tone tentative. "It was after the royal race. Most people stayed outside but some wandered back into the box. I was out on the deck but happened to look behind me … and noticed my mother and Lord Barchester talking."

He paused again, loyalty clearly waging battle with honesty. Dodo felt a desire to bang her head on the cabinet wall.

"Sounds innocent enough. She was the host," encouraged Charlie.

"This was no small-talk, Charlie. It was intense—not the kind of conversation strangers engage in. Mother told *me* they had only met once before at the dinner she held…but I think she might be lying."

Dodo squeezed Charlie's wrist. *More romantic intrigue? What did people see in the man?*

"What else happened?" said Charlie.

"Nothing. It was a very short conversation as Lady Barchester walked back inside and they pulled apart instantly. That image alone was worth a thousand words. If it was innocent, why not carry on talking? I cannot get it out of my head."

"Have you talked to her about it?" asked Charlie.

"It's Mater, old chap! How would one go about that? Hello, Mother. Tell me, were you having a relationship with the late Lord Barchester? I can barely even say it out loud."

Dodo could imagine his cheeks flaming to match his ginger hair.

"Yes, I see your point. Jolly awkward," Charlie agreed.

Dodo had an idea and whispered in Charlie's ear.

"Would you like *me* to tell the chief inspector, and see if he thinks it is worth following up on?" Charlie asked.

A whooshing sound down the line indicated the release of nervous tension. "Would you, old chap? I'd be very grateful. It seems so disloyal if I do it, do you see?"

"Of course. I'll tell him it's an anonymous tip if you like?"

"There! I knew you would know how to handle it!" They could hear Alistair clearing his throat. "It could get so dashed embarrassing, and I don't want to rock the family boat if I can help it."

"Think nothing of it," Charlie assured him. "I'll make sure the chief inspector knows. He will probably re-interview your mother, but I'm sure he will be very discreet."

"You're the best!" Alistair said in a breathy voice. "Oh, I can hear someone coming. Toodle-pip!"

The line went dead.

"People are so unpredictable," gasped Dodo. "Everyone has secrets. Everyone."

"Do you?" asked Charlie.

Dodo looked down at her knees, cramped next to his, so that he could not read her expression.

Time to deflect the conversation.

She raised her patented smile. "Alistair's mother and Lord Barchester. She's so…"

"Unattractive?" he finished.

"I suppose it's no stranger than Lord Barchester and Felicity?"

"I suppose not. We're getting a rather different picture of him though."

"Well, that's what happens during an investigation. It's like a jigsaw puzzle but the box of pieces has been scattered and you have to search for every one. As you discover them, they build a true picture of the victim."

"Yes, and he was a thoroughly rotten philanderer."

Charlie would never do such a thing. Loyalty and honor radiated from the man.

"It would seem so…" she began.

The phone rang with an ear-splitting sound in the tiny box, scaring them both.

Charlie picked up the earpiece again. "Chadwick Hall."

"I'm calling for Lady Dorothea Dorchester. She gave me this number."

"Of course. Hold on one moment." Charlie had imitated his butler to perfection catching Dodo off-guard. She felt an adolescent desire to shriek with laughter but smashed her lips together to prevent it.

Charlie handed her the phone, his eyes dancing with mischief.

She waited a suitable time before answering. "This is Lady Dorothea."

"It's David."

Dorothea's eyes widened and she stared at Charlie with meaning.

"David! Did you discover something already?"

"Yes. It didn't take long actually. Turns out your Lord Barchester was a bit of a rake. Seems he made passes at most of the secretaries in the typing pool. They even had a nickname for him; Bawdy Barchester."

Dodo flapped her hands. "David, you are so clever!"

"I'd like to take credit, but the facts practically fell into my lap. He was so bad, the girls warned any new female employees about him and how to avoid his unwanted advances. They had a celebration when he left."

"This is marvelous information. We are building a rather unflattering image of the man and this confirms it."

"The wedding is the fourteenth of next month, by the way," David said with a lilt.

"I'll be there. Thank you!" She replaced the receiver. "Did you hear all that?"

"Something about a wedding?"

Dodo punched him in the arm.

"That is the 'payment'," she said with a smile. "You don't mind, do you? David's just an old friend." She puckered her lips.

Charlie's eyes fixed on them and he pressed a hungry kiss to her mouth.

"Mind? I'm eaten up with jealousy."

"David's mother gives him a bad time if he turns up to family weddings without a female in tow."

"It will be a sore trial, but I will fall on my sword to make the sacrifice…for the case." Charlie quirked an eyebrow.

"Thank you. Now, did you hear the other stuff?" she asked.

"Bawdy Barchester?" said Charlie with an impish grin.

"So, you did hear." Her lips twisted wickedly.

"I always pay attention to alliteration." A choirboy could not have looked more innocent.

Dodo rolled her eyes as Charlie opened the door to the telephone cabinet, and they peeled out.

"All this information makes it more likely that he was killed by a jealous boyfriend, husband or a woman scorned," he declared.

"It also begs the question, 'Who else there that day did Lord Barchester have a secret history with?' Felicity and Mrs. Guthrie for sure. What about Portia?"

Charlie let out a guffaw. "Not a chance! She's much too sensible."

"The only other woman there was the colonel's wife." Dodo's mouth dropped open. Then in tandem they shook their heads.

"No way. Much too old," said Charlie.

Dodo arched a brow, tapping her lips with a finger. "There is one other possibility."

Charlie tipped his head to one side. "Who?"

"The wait staff. There were two young women overseeing the food. I didn't pay attention to either of them but perhaps Lord Barchester did—given his reputation."

"His predatory behavior with women gives his wife the strongest motive," Charlie mused.

"I would agree except for the fact that she is dead. And why is she dead? A jealous husband would have no beef with her, as far as I can see."

Charlie nodded. "Yes, that does put a wrench in my theory."

His head snapped up. "This will make today's interview of the Guthrie's all the more interesting."

"Oh yes. Might make it a bit tricky. Perhaps we should get Mrs. Guthrie alone?" The woman was unlikely to talk of indiscretions in the presence of her husband.

Charlie lifted a finger. "I happen to know she takes the dogs for a long walk on the land around their estate around eleven every day. Perhaps we could bump into her with my dogs if we leave now."

"That's a marvelous idea, Charlie."

"You should call the chief inspector before we leave, and I'll tell mother that we are taking the dogs." His voice trailed off as he hurried away.

Charlie revealed no residual envy over the encounter with the chief inspector the day before. His trust in her was absolute. *Did she deserve it?*

She went back inside the telephone cabinet.

Steeling herself, she picked up the receiver. Her heart was beating erratically, and her hands were sweaty.

"Scotland Yard please," she told the operator in a firm voice.

All her muscles tensed.

"Blood." He snapped the word into the phone.

Dodo reared back at his abrupt tone. "Hello, Chief Inspector, it's Dodo Dorchester."

"Oh, sorry." His voice immediately lost its edge. "What can I do for you?" A vision of his square jaw and russet eyes burst into her mind. She shooed it away.

She filled him in on Alistair's phone call and his request that everything be very discreet, and then explained that they had thought of a way to intercept Mrs. Guthrie while she was alone.

"Very resourceful," commented the chief inspector.

Then she laid out the things David had discovered, adding their conclusions about the staff.

"Well, well. That is a surprise." He paused. "We questioned the maids at the time, and they gave no indication that he had messed with them. For once he may have been on his best behavior."

"Apparently so."

He paused again. Should she end the call?

"I went to see the colonel and his wife yesterday evening … after you left," he said.

"Oh. Did you learn anything?"

"I confirmed that the colonel did serve in Burma. Received a medal for heroic action under fire. Went out a lance corporal and came back a sergeant. Just as he said."

"Do you see any connection with Lord Barchester?"

"Not at the present. But I am looking into the victim's service record. Perhaps their paths crossed over there? I'm having to tread very carefully. Questioning a member of the Prime Minister's cabinet will not win me any friends. I could lose my job if it goes south."

"Yes, I can see that," she replied thoughtfully. "Are you working under the assumption that both murders were committed by the same person?"

"I try not to make assumptions, Lady Dorothea. But before your call, I was leaning in that direction. Now we know of Lord Barchester's indecent tendencies…I just don't know. But if his murder *was* linked to his behavior, why kill his wife?"

"I have been plagued with the same question. The only thing I can come up with is that perhaps she saw the murderer fleeing and didn't tell you?"

"That seems unlikely, but it is one solution."

"Or the murderer feared he told his wife something before he died that incriminated them?" Her breath had made a misty mark on the window of the cabinet and she dragged her finger through it.

"Yeees. That's more plausible."

Another pause. Part of her wanted to keep him on the line, but it was time to go.

"I'll contact you after we talk to Mrs. Guthrie. Good day, Chief Inspector."

"Good day, Lady Dorothea."

She hung up. Her heart hammering.

Why did he have this effect on her? And why did it bother her so much that he refused to call her Dodo?

As she exited the booth, her eye caught on the mark she had made with her finger.

It was a heart.

Chapter 13

Dogs are always eager for an outing and Charlie's were no exception. They readily jumped into his battered car, drooling over Dodo's shoulder the entire drive. Fortunately, it wasn't too far.

"Mrs. Guthrie walks this way every day with her dogs," Charlie explained as they all tumbled out. "I went with her a couple of times. I suggest we wait here and watch for them. I brought some binoculars. Once we see her, we can set off so it will appear as if we've met by chance."

Charlie was wearing a smashing, flat cap that added greatly to his appeal, and tan trousers with a light sweater. She was becoming very fond of that captivating smile, which caused a twinge of self-reproach.

He handed Dodo the binoculars and she scanned the meadows. In the distance she could see a church steeple and a slight depression crowded with a tangle of little thatched cottages. Swinging the lenses around, the landscape leveled out with fields of brown and white dairy cows and trees in a line, signaling the presence of a stream.

Though the day was generally overcast, the sun poked through the clouds every few minutes ensuring a pleasant temperature and forming a patchwork of flickering light over the fields. They leaned against a gate checking for Mrs. Guthrie every few minutes.

"What did the chief inspector have to say?" Charlie asked, keeping his eyes to the lenses.

She told him the latest.

"Burma. I've been thinking a lot about that since Portia mentioned it. I swept the deepest recesses of my mind and came up with some vague memories from school history lessons. I believe there was a skirmish there between the locals and us."

"Really? I have absolutely no clue. I find history an absolute bore, quite frankly," she replied.

"That's because schools just teach long lists of dates and names." He dropped the binoculars so that they hung on the strap around his neck. "I had a marvelous history teacher—full of enthusiasm and tales about actual people."

"It was called the Anglo-Burmese War and it stretched from the mid 1880's to the mid 1890's. The natives were not in favor of British occupation. If I remember correctly, there was some burning and pillaging of villages by our boys. Not Britain's finest hour."

Dodo turned around to watch the progress of a pretty songbird. "But what would that have to do with the here and now?"

"I can't imagine." He lifted the binoculars once more. "We're up! Mrs. Guthrie is headed this way. Let's walk away from her, but slowly, so that she catches up with us."

"You have a brilliantly devious mind, Mr. Chadwick."

He honored her with another of his stunning smiles and she felt her heart catch as he offered her his arm.

Charlie called to the dogs who were sniffing around the trees, and they all began to walk away from Mrs. Guthrie as if they had not seen her.

"Remind me what we need to ask her?" asked Charlie.

"How could you forget? Remember, Alistair thinks she is lying about only just meeting Lord Barchester and that something was going on between the pair of them. We need to poke around a bit. It's going to take some fancy footwork."

"Oh yes. I think I'll leave that part to you. I'll butter her up with some small talk."

Strolling at a very leisurely pace, Dodo risked a cautious look behind her.

"Not long now," she warned.

Within a couple of minutes Mrs. Guthrie was upon them, about to walk right past when she happened to glance at their way.

"Well, I never!" she exclaimed, her wild, red curls bouncing around as she spoke. "Charlie and Dorothea." She looked at their interlocked arms and gave a knowing smile. "What are you two doing in my neck of the woods?"

Charlie answered. "I remember walking the dogs with you when I was staying at the house and thought it would be a walk that Dodo might appreciate."

Mrs. Guthrie looked from one to the other with a slight frown. Dodo arranged her features into her most innocent expression.

"And how do you like it?" Her prominent teeth gleamed in the sun, framed by her expansive lips.

"It's absolutely beautiful," said Dodo, using all her drama class skills to transform her countenance appropriately.

"It is a lovely part of the country." Her smile could not have been brighter had her dogs just won best in show.

The hounds were happily sniffing each other. With her eyes suddenly fixed on the dogs, Mrs. Guthrie asked, "Have you heard any more about the murder?"

"I believe Scotland Yard has made some progress," said Dodo.

"That's what they always say. Means they have nothing." Mrs. Guthrie puffed air through her lips causing her hair to flap.

"Well, it's been lovely seeing you…" she made motions indicating that she was about to race off.

Time for drastic measures.

"Did the chief inspector tell you that Lady Barchester has been murdered too?"

Mrs. Guthrie's head jerked up, her pale complexion drained completely, her eyes frantic. "What did you say?"

"They've kept it out of the papers so far, but I thought the chief inspector might have told you. Lady Barchester was killed the day after her husband died."

Mrs. Guthrie's knees buckled.

What is causing such an excessive reaction?

"I say, are you alright?" Charlie asked as Mrs. Guthrie wobbled.

"I think I'm feeling a bit wonky, actually." Beads of perspiration had broken out on her upper lip.

"Here let's sit on this wooden stile." Charlie gripped Mrs. Guthrie's hand and helped her sit down.

As they watched, Mrs. Guthrie began rocking, biting her lip.

"Can I run and get you something?" Charlie asked.

Mrs. Guthrie's eyes were crowded with hidden secrets that were clearly tormenting her. Dodo crouched down to wrap her arms around Mrs. Guthrie as though she were a child. The dogs, sensing something amiss with their mistress, came to lay at her feet. Mrs. Guthrie leaned into Dodo and closed her eyes, deep wrinkles appearing at the edges.

Were these exaggerated emotions evidence of a deeper guilt than they had imagined?

After several minutes passed, she seemed to gather up the tatters of her emotional strength enough to withdraw from Dodo's embrace.

She put a hand to her clammy cheek. "Heavens, what must you think of me?"

"I'm terribly sorry that we shocked you," began Dodo. "I didn't realize that you were that close to Lady Barchester."

"Oh, I'm not," Mrs. Guthrie said. "It's just so … unexpected."

"It's a complication for the police as they always seem to suspect the spouse first in crimes of this nature," Dodo said.

"Logical thinking, I suppose," said Mrs. Guthrie, her voice delicate and fragile. "How…?"

"Poison," revealed Dodo. "In her tea."

Mrs. Guthrie's hand went to her mouth.

"This does seem to have affected you a great deal," Charlie said.

Mrs. Guthrie opened and closed her mouth several times as if to speak, reminding Dodo of a big, orange goldfish.

Finally, she appeared to scrape together her courage. "I wasn't exactly forthcoming with the chief inspector," she began, pursing her lips. "I told him that I did not know Lord Barchester very well … but that is not strictly true." A redness began creeping up her neck like a rash.

Here we go.

Though Dodo's mind was racing with a million questions for Mrs. Guthrie, she dug her nails into her palms to keep herself from scaring the woman into silence. This was the part of interviewing that was a balance of skill and patience.

Mrs. Guthrie tipped back her head as though needing to draw additional strength from the sky. "We met, as I said, at an event and Lord Barchester and I hit it off."

She stopped and glanced at Dodo.

"I hope you won't think less of me, Lady Dorothea?"

Saying nothing, Dodo reached out and touched her hand.

"I decided to invite him to our dinner party and at the end of the evening he told me about a little place he liked to go in the City. He invited me to join him there the following evening…alone. He said he would appreciate my help in navigating his new role as an earl. I didn't see any harm in it." The shame radiating from her face said otherwise.

"We had a lovely meal and he asked me all sorts of questions about high society and then I left, but not before he asked if he could see me again. I was flattered and we met up several times a week in the run up to Ascot. It was just a little fling you understand. A bit of fun. No funny business. He was the perfect gentleman." She put her fingers to her temples and sighed.

"As you can imagine I was shocked more than most when he was killed, but it wasn't like I was in love with him or anything. So, I didn't think the chief inspector needed to know about our harmless trysts. It might look like I had a motive."

Perhaps Lord Barchester wanted more and threatened to tell your husband.

Mrs. Guthrie suddenly clasped her stringy neck.

"Arthur was not there!" She shrieked, shocking Dodo to her core.

"What?" asked Dodo, confused.

"I'm just putting two and two together." She dragged frantic fingers through her hair. "When we arrived home after the races, as Arthur was coming out of the bathroom, I remembered that he came through the door of the box from the stairs at some point before the screaming. I filed the memory away as unimportant. The trauma of the murder must have made me forget at the time I was questioned."

The woman was babbling, not making any sense.

She grabbed Dodo by the shoulders her eyes crazed and bloodshot. "Now that you have told me about Lady Barchester, I am realizing that Arthur was gone before the murder *and* he was gone all the next day! What if he found out about Lord Barchester and killed him in a fit of jealousy? And then killed Lady Barchester thinking that she saw him?"

Chapter 14

Mr. Guthrie? A murderer?

As experienced as Dodo now was in sleuthing, she had to admit that Mrs. Guthrie's admissions and suspicions had blindsided her.

Imagining the eccentric woman in the role of philanderer still took some getting used to and casting her forgettable husband as the vigilante? Well, it beggared belief.

It was infuriating that people were generally so dishonest with the police—even those with nothing to hide. If Mrs. Guthrie had told all this to the chief inspector at the outset, their investigations would have taken a completely different route and possibly saved the life of Lady Barchester. The thought filled her with anger.

It had taken some time, but they had finally convinced Mrs. Guthrie to telephone the chief inspector. Would he be as surprised as she?

They walked her back to the house under a cloud and Charlie and Dodo waited in the drawing room while she made the call.

Anxiety was stamped all over Mrs. Guthrie's face as she staggered back into the room.

"The chief inspector was very angry," she moaned. "He's coming right over. To question Arthur."

Doubts about the wisdom of her confession were clearly threatening to overwhelm her. Suddenly it was as if a cloth had abruptly wiped those apprehensions away as her face stiffened with a new fear.

"What if Arthur discovers *I* am the one who informed on him?"

Was there more to Mr. Guthrie than met the eye?

"Is your husband prone to violence?" Dodo asked.

"No. Not at all." Her face became wistful. "For all his faults, he has never been violent."

"Then you have nothing to fear," Dodo said. "I expect the chief inspector will say that a witness has come forward who remembers your husband leaving the box around the time of the murder and simply ask him to account for it."

"Oh, but I do! I am completely hopeless at concealing my feelings. It's why I don't play cards. If I have to sit here and pretend it wasn't me, I shall break down. I'll have to leave before the chief inspector gets here."

Wringing her hands, she spluttered, "I shall have to go shopping."

Dodo thought this might be a euphemism for going straight to the pub.

"Where is your husband now?" asked Charlie.

"Checking on the tenants. One of them reported a leaky roof."

"Can you be sure he will be back this afternoon?" Dodo asked.

With confidence she declared, "Oh, yes. He's a creature of habit. He always comes home for lunch. Like clockwork."

"You've done the right thing," Dodo assured her. "It would be impossible to live with this level of suspicion. Now you will know one way or the other. And the Barchesters deserve justice—wherever that may lead."

Mrs. Guthrie's pacing was threatening to wear out the pattern on the carpet. "It is so sordid. What will people say?"

"Have you considered that he might be innocent? Your husband may have a perfectly credible alibi," Dodo pointed out.

Mrs. Guthrie stopped pacing, her eyes strained and bloodshot. "But what if it *was* him?"

"Then he must be brought to justice," Dodo said gently. "No one is above the law Mrs. Guthrie and two people have been murdered."

"I suppose when you put it like that…" Her hands were trembling.

"Let me get you something to calm those nerves," said Charlie. Mrs. Guthrie waved to the drinks cabinet and Charlie poured her a stiff brandy.

As she tipped it down her throat in one gulp, her eyes screwed up as it burned its way down. She placed the tumbler on the coffee table and leaned back, her face crumpled with grief.

"It's like being thrust into the middle of a ghastly nightmare," she moaned. "When will I wake up?"

Dodo heard the clock in the hall chime twelve-thirty. "What time do you usually have lunch?"

"One."

"Then you should gather your things and get ready to leave," Dodo said. "We can drop you somewhere and you can get a taxi home later. How does that sound?"

Her face full of relief, she nodded. "Let me grab my handbag. I'll be right back."

Considering what they had learned about Mr. Guthrie, Dodo wondered if Mrs. Guthrie would ever go home again.

***

They managed to make their escape well before Mr. Guthrie's return and squashed Mrs. Guthrie into the back of the old, black Ford, beside the two panting Labradors.

Dropping her in the middle of the closest town, Dodo watched as she walked straight past the dress shop she had mentioned, to the pub on the other side. Dodo could not imagine the stress of thinking that your husband might be a double murderer. Mrs. Guthrie would have a whopper of a hangover the next morning.

As soon as Mrs. Guthrie was out of earshot, a low rumble started in Charlie's chest that bubbled up and spilled out as raucous laughter.

"I can see the appeal of this line of work," Charlie managed to blurt out between convulsions. "It can be quite entertaining...better than the movies. Who would have ever cast her in the role of femme fatale?" He wiped the tears from the corners of his eyes.

"Charlie," she said with a heavy dose of reproach. "The poor woman is beside herself. But I agree, it is hard to imagine."

"So, the case could be closed as early as this evening," remarked Charlie once he had his laughter under control.

"You think Mr. Guthrie did it? Killed Lord Barchester and then went to tea with Lady Barchester and poisoned her?"

"Don't you? This new evidence is pretty compelling."

"I don't know," Dodo said. "It's all rather circumstantial at this point. Nothing solid."

Charlie engaged the gears and eased out into traffic.

"Shall we go out for dinner?" he said. "I know a little place in the shadow of the palace in Windsor that sits just by the river."

"Sounds perfect."

***

Soaking in a perfumed bath before dinner was one of life's little pleasures that Dodo clung to. Even at someone else's house and especially in the middle of a case. It helped organize her thoughts.

And something about Mr. Guthrie being the murderer did not feel right. She ran through the list of other suspects.

Felicity had explained her association with Lord Barchester, and unless she was lying, it amounted to very little. And, according to her, Alexander was ignorant of all of it. So, unless he had risen up against a member of the aristocracy for political motives, he seemed an unlikely candidate.

Sally, the barmaid, had corroborated Alistair's alibi and the police had followed up on her claim that she had won some money on a race, and Portia and Roger had no connection to Lord Barchester apparently only meeting him that very day.

She turned her thoughts to the older people. The colonel and Lord Barchester had both served in the army. Was this significant? Had they served in the same area of Burma? She still didn't know. And as an important and influential member of the Prime Minister's cabinet, Colonel Winchester could ill afford to get involved in a murder scandal that could lead to the end of his career. Mrs. Winchester was an ambitious woman who basked in the reflected glory of her husband's career. She would be unlikely to endanger it. And though Lord Barchester had proven to be a ladies' man, it seemed unlikely that he would have dallied with such an exceptionally plain woman, ten years his senior, even if he did have a flirtation with the horsey Mrs. Guthrie.

And then there was the problem of the note. They still didn't know who'd given Lord Barchester the blasted thing. This was the one piece of evidence that seemed to prove that someone had pre-meditated his murder. Was he a threat or was it a crime of revenge? Without this knowledge they were at an impasse. And why kill his wife? Had she unwittingly glimpsed the killer as Dodo was beginning to believe?

Dodo sighed and sank lower in the fragrant water.

Then there was the problem of Charlie. How did she feel about him? Was it fair to lead him on when she was so confused? And what about Chief Inspector Blood? Was it time to examine her feelings about the man? Would she seriously consider a relationship with the chief inspector if they were equals socially? It was an uncomfortable question and she shrunk from the answer.

In frustration, Dodo sank beneath the water and blew bubbles out of her nose.

***

Dodo examined her hair in the dressing table mirror. Lizzie, Dodo's lady's maid, had not been able to come with her to Chadwick Hall as her sister was getting married. Lizzie knew just how to style her hair. The Chadwick's maid had done a fair job, but it wasn't quite how she liked it. The new bob cut could be tricky to dress.

She missed Lizzie.

She rolled her eyes at her reflection and shook her head.

A soft knock on her door interrupted her musings and she opened it to find Charlie, eyes gleaming like the summer sky. A seed of guilt fell into the soft soil of her harrowed conscience.

"Your carriage awaits, m'lady."

***

The restaurant had strung some outdoor lighting that reminded Dodo of the bistros in Paris. Flower baskets hung on hooks from the walls and along the fence by the water. They opted to sit outside and watch the river roll by with the great walls of Windsor Castle providing a dramatic backdrop. The light rain that had passed, gave the air an earthy, midsummer fragrance.

While they were waiting for their food, Charlie took Dodo's hand across the table.

"Dodo, I've been thinking…"

Oh no.

The fact that this was her first thought was worrisome.

"I've really enjoyed these last few days…" His smile was slow but striking. "I was hoping we could make it a bit official."

"Official?" She gulped, a storm stirring inside her.

"Yes, I'd like to ask you to be my girlfriend."

Phew! The emotional storm calmed.

She could do that. *Why had she imagined he was going to propose?*

"I thought that's what I was?"

He rubbed his thumb along hers. "Well, we've just been friends for so many years that the lines kind of got blurred. I just wanted to clarify things." His eyes searched her face. "So, I can call you my girlfriend? When you go home tomorrow, I can come and visit and take you out whenever I want?"

This uncertain side of Charlie was new to Dodo.

"I would like that," she murmured and as she said it, she realized it was true.

"Dodo." His voice was husky, ripe with emotion. "I want to see where this goes."

She threaded her fingers through his. "Me too."

"I have another year left at Cambridge for my bachelor's but if I want to be a professor, I will have to begin a master's program right away. I can work as a tutor while I study. Once I begin work on my PhD, I can begin teaching. It's not glamorous but it's honest work. And I'll have an allowance of course." Charlie was the second son and would not inherit his father's estate. He was wondering if he was enough.

Why?

"Let's take things one day at a time," she said.

"But I—"

The waiter's return interrupted him, for which she was grateful.

She had ordered grilled halibut in a white wine sauce with asparagus. She dug in her fork proclaiming the fish divine to prevent Charlie picking up the thread of his conversation.

Charlie looked down at his food, but his gaze was unfocused.

As Dodo took her second bite, a woman at a table across the patio squealed like a stuck pig. A flash of memory brought back the colonel's unusual laugh as he sat with all the young people the day of the race.

Time to steer the dangerous conversation back to the murder.

"Gosh! What a terrible laugh," she declared. "I thought someone was hurt. Remember the colonel's eccentric laugh?"

Charlie nodded. "Yes, it sounded like a wild animal was in the room."

Dodo slammed her silverware down. "What if his laugh was so unique that it reminded Lord Barchester of something that happened a long time ago? What if they did serve together in the Far East, in Burma, but they didn't recognize each other after all these years? What if something happened that the colonel would rather keep quiet?"

"But the colonel never left the box. His hip," Charlie pointed out.

Dodo blew air out of her mouth in frustration. "Drat! You're right."

"And it's quite possible that it was Mr. Guthrie who murdered Lord Barchester. Until the chief inspector has laid that theory to rest, why pursue other lines of investigation?"

She wasn't sure she agreed but was in no mood to argue the point. The discussion had led away from the tricky declaration he seemed poised to make and that was enough for now.

The fact that the two men may have known each other in the past was difficult to ignore. She would make plans to look into their history at a later time, alone if necessary.

Chapter 15

"Darlings!" Dodo's mother, Lady Guinevere Dorchester floated toward them in a flowing kimono, hands outstretched. "Charlie dear, you look simply delicious." She kissed him on both cheeks as they stood in the tiled entryway, and then studied Dodo's face. Dodo felt as though her mother was reading her soul.

Charlie had driven Dodo home and thankfully the conversation had been less serious than the one the previous evening.

"Tell me you're staying for lunch, darling," said Lady Guinevere to Charlie.

He looked to Dodo who nodded. "Of course, he is."

"Goody," said Guinevere, threading her arm through Charlie's and leading them out onto the patio where a big umbrella provided shade and a frosty jug of lemonade sat with a tumbler, next to a copy of *Country Life* magazine.

"Sit, sit." She went to the glass doors. "Cartwright! Be a darling and bring us two more tumblers."

Dodo hid a smile as she imagined Cartwright's horror at being called a 'darling' by his mistress.

Lady Guinevere sat. "Now dears, tell me all about your adventures."

Dodo knew that her mother avoided any disturbing news and only read the society pages of the newspaper. Would the murder have been mentioned? He was a lord after all.

"Do you remember ever meeting a Lord Barchester, Mummy?"

Her mother's lips puckered in thought. "Barchester? Barchester?"

His name didn't ring any bells then. "I believe you met him and his wife a couple of months ago at some dinner party. He was new to the title."

Her mother frowned. "What does he look like?"

"Medium height and build, salt and pepper hair. Mid-fifties. A rather plain wife with a lot to learn about how to dress—"

"Ah, now I remember! He was a little frisky." She patted the side of her nose with a finger.

"That's him," confirmed Dodo.

Guinevere poured herself some more lemonade. "What about him?"

"He's dead."

Her mother's head jolted back as though she had been lassoed. "Oh Dodo! Not again! I don't know how I feel about you being involved in all these murders. It is so"—she searched the air for the right word—"vulgar, darling."

"I am not *involved*, Mummy. I help bring the criminals to justice. That's a *good* thing." Dodo exchanged a look of longsuffering with Charlie.

"I'd much rather you didn't, dear. It's so unsettling." Guinevere turned to Charlie searching for an ally. "Don't you agree, Charlie?"

"Actually, I rather admire the way her brain works." He grinned, revealing a hidden dimple she had not noticed till now.

"She needs no encouragement," declared Lady Guinevere turning back to her daughter. "Why can't you take up tennis or sailing or some other innocuous hobby?"

There was no answer to this. Instead, Dodo rested her chin in her hand. "Do you want to know what happened, or not?"

"Well, of course I do since you are involved," Guinevere conceded, "but spare me the gory details. I haven't had lunch."

No time would be the right time for gruesome details where her mother was concerned.

Dodo summarized what had happened as a servant brought out more glasses. Her mother poured them a drink, while Dodo continued her story leaving out the fact that Lady Barchester had also been murdered. One murder was quite enough.

"That was a short-lived earldom, then. How shocking. Do you have any idea who might have done it?"

One of the Dorchester's dogs ambled over from soaking up the sun to see if there were any scraps to be had. Guinevere picked him up and ruffled the fur around his collar. He looked up at her with unadulterated adoration.

"I had some ideas but no facts, as yet, and then yesterday, a stunning admission turned everything on its head."

"How so?" Both the lap dog and her mother cocked their heads at Dodo in unison.

"Mrs. Guthrie—the hostess at Ascot—admitted to an indiscretion with the former Lord Barchester and suspected that her husband may have heard about it and wreaked his revenge."

Guinevere stared wide-eyed. "This sounds like one of those badly written detective novels."

Charlie laughed. "That is a very perceptive observation, Lady Guinevere."

Dodo crossed her arms on the table. "Until the chief inspector gets to the bottom of that wrinkle, there's really no point working on any other suspicions. If it does turn out to be him then the case is closed."

But I do feel the need to satisfy my own curiosity about Burma.

Lady Guinevere put her hand to her chest. "My pulse is racing just thinking about it. I don't know how you cope with the stress."

Since her mother was so squeamish concerning murder, Dodo decided it was time to turn to less alarming topics. Her mother's knowledge of people was bordering on encyclopedic and Dodo wanted to know what she knew about Colonel and Mrs. Winchester.

She reached out to tickle the dog. "Do you know Colonel Winchester or his wife, Mummy? He's on the Prime Minister's cabinet."

"Winchester? Yes, I've attended various functions where they were guests. I wouldn't say I *know* them. But I believe Granny does."

Granny was the Dowager, Lord Dorchester's mother.

"I think I'll have a chat with her then."

"Why?"

"Oh, the colonel was one of the guests at Ascot and someone mentioned that he served in the Far East…Burma. I was interested, that's all."

The butler appeared in the French window frame. "Luncheon is served, your ladyship."

"Oh Cartwright, I've changed my mind. I want to eat out here."

The only indication that the butler was annoyed by this last-minute change of plans was a slightly deeper intake of breath before he spoke. "As you wish, your ladyship."

***

Charlie left after lunch, but not without kissing Dodo completely and thoroughly and arranging a time to take her out later in the week.

Dodo went in search of Lizzie.

She found her in the kitchen having a cup of tea with the cook and the maids. All the servants rushed to their feet as Dodo entered.

"Do sit down," she insisted. "Lizzie do you have a moment?"

Lizzie had become Dodo's lady's maid at seventeen having been trained from the age of fourteen for the position. Dodo had been fifteen. Over the years Lizzie had become more of a confidant and friend than a mere servant.

Once they got up to Dodo's bedroom, Dodo hugged her. "How was the wedding?"

"It was lovely, and Ginny looked a peach."

Dodo asked for all the details and Lizzie was happy to oblige. There were eight children in Lizzie's family and five of them were girls. Ginny was the third oldest and first to get married.

"And what about you?" exclaimed Lizzie. "I read about the murder of course."

Dodo took great delight in relating all the sordid details—except that Chief Inspector Blood was the detective assigned to the case. Lizzie had helped Dodo in several cases and was a fount of common sense.

"So, *you* don't think it's Mr. Guthrie?" she said.

Dodo's mouth twisted. "No. It doesn't feel...right. And this war in the Far East keeps niggling at me."

"I'm sure you'll connect the dots in the end. You always do. Now," said Lizzie sitting on the chintz armchair, her face flushed with anticipation. "Tell me everything about Mr. Charlie."

Dodo told her all about the lovely week she had spent with him and then laid out her dilemma, omitting the complication of the chief inspector.

"The crux of the matter is whether I'm leading Charlie on?"

"You're still young m'lady. Plenty of time for shopping around before settling down. You don't believe he's thinking of popping the question, do you?"

"Heavens no! It's only been a week. Though I did worry about that last night when we were at the restaurant."

"Then I think you're fine. Just because the sky doesn't explode every time you're with him right now, doesn't mean it won't happen later. Relationships grow or they die. It takes time to see which way things will go. You want someone constant to have a nice time with."

Dodo wondered if Lizzie was thinking of the charismatic but unreliable Frenchman who had almost broken Dodo's heart in Paris.

"When did you get so wise?" Dodo asked her.

"When my school friend Jenny got married at sixteen to her sweetheart and he left her with a baby after a year. She was besotted with him and look where that left her. Ginny's new husband is the steady kind. She knows she can always count on him. Not much of a looker, but reliable."

As Lizzie talked, Dodo's anxiousness began to slip away. "Thank you, Lizzie, I feel a lot better."

"Think nothing of it m'lady." She stood to leave. "Oh, and the Dowager is coming to dinner tonight. We got the call just before you came down to the kitchen."

Perfect!

***

Granny Dorchester was a favorite of Dodo's. Though she had grown up in the last century under strict Victorian morality, she was a surprisingly forward thinker and often supported Dodo in her riskier adventures.

The family had finished the first two courses of dinner and were awaiting dessert. They had exhausted all the small talk and permissible gossip and Dodo was waiting for an opening to question her grandmother about Burma.

Her parents started to discuss a housekeeping matter, and Dodo seized the opportunity. She dropped her voice. "Granny, did you know I was at Ascot the day of the murder?"

With a twinkle in her eye the Dowager replied, "Of course, why do you think I'm here?"

"I'll tell you all the juicy details after dinner in the drawing room, but I do have one question. The victim may have served in Burma along with one of the other guests. It's quite a coincidence."

"Burma? That would have been in the 1880's. I was in my forties then. Let me have a little think while we eat dessert and we can discuss it in the drawing room."

Dessert was a delicious apple charlotte made with delicate French finger cakes doused in a calvados sauce. It took all Dodo's concentration.

After dinner she and her grandmother retreated to a corner of the large drawing room and Dodo again laid out the case in exquisite detail. As so often happens when one is retelling a story, a forgotten memory was triggered, and she recalled being bumped on the shoulder as they went out onto the deck, right before the body was found. She squeezed her eyes shut and tried to tease the image back. She had barely looked back at the culprit at the time but now remembered the sense that it was a short, stubby man. Only one person fit the bill – Mr. Guthrie. Mrs. Guthrie must have got her times wrong! His wife was afraid that she saw him entering the door from the stairs at the same time he knocked Dodo coming through the door *from* the deck. This fact would account for the unsettled feeling Dodo had experienced since he had become the main suspect.

She would have to tell the chief inspector as soon as possible.

"Remembered something important?" asked the Dowager, her crystal earring glinting in the light.

"Yes, but never mind that now." Dodo wanted to keep to the matter at hand before Granny became too tired.

The Dowager took a sip of her sherry. "Now who is it that was in Burma, dear?" Her grandmother's papery skin draped as she tipped her head in query.

"Lord Barchester, who would have been plain Jeremy Barchester, and Colonel Winchester. I believe his name is Cuthbert. They would both have been young men back then. Mummy says you might know the colonel."

"The one in the Prime Minister's cabinet?" The Dowager's jowls wobbled with interest.

"The very same."

"Yes, I know him. But I have to say that he's one of those people who rub me the wrong way. There's something lacking in his manners in my opinion and he has a tendency to drop into vulgarity which is quite unbecoming. I was quite shocked when the Prime Minister picked him for his cabinet. And his wife…she's a social climber of the worst kind."

"That was my impression too, Granny." She scooted closer to her grandmother. "I think both men may have served in that war. I'm trying to discover if there is any connection. At Ascot it appeared that they were meeting for the first time. I think that might not be the case. So, what do you know about that war?"

"I've been trying to remember," began the Dowager. "The first battle was quickly won, but I recall your grandfather saying that mistakes were made and promises broken and the natives became angry which led to uprisings for the next ten years or so. Sir Henry Prendergast was the commander. Your grandfather had no time for him. He was a boorish, unpleasant man. I recall that your grandfather was disgusted by reports of looting and the killing of innocent villagers. He said the British should be above such sordid practices and it was a stain on the whole Empire."

War crimes?

"Your grandfather seemed to think some rather shady things went on under his command, things that would never have happened if the soldiers were in England. Lawlessness and that kind of thing. He was particularly interested in it all because our housekeeper's sister lost a son over there. What was his name? Haversham? Haversmith?" She snapped her fingers. "Haviland! That's it. Matthew Haviland. He was a young man in his twenties and the loss hit them hard. He was their only child, a young private who had only been out for a few months. Mrs. Nibley, my housekeeper, told me that he was a well-liked boy with an unusual laugh."

Interest stirred in Dodo. "Unusual how?"

"I remember it because the housekeeper imitated it one day. It was a cross between a hyena and a donkey."

Chapter 16

Dodo's brain started firing on all pistons.

"Colonel Winchester has a laugh one might describe like that. It caught the attention of everyone in the room."

"Well, *I've* heard the colonel laugh and it most definitely is *not* like that," contradicted her grandmother. "It's more of a guffaw."

"I was there Granny. One short honking sound and then his wife reprimanded him." Dodo's head hurt as it tried to make sense out of things.

"Perhaps he was imitating someone?" offered the Dowager.

"Perhaps. Where was the young man from? The one who died?"

"Northampton, if memory serves. Why?"

"It may be nothing, but it might be a lead." *However flimsy.* "I don't suppose any of those people are still alive?"

"My old housekeeper, Mrs. Nibley was his aunt. Do you remember her? She's in a boarding house in Lancing."

Dodo remembered a little lady with a big personality.

"I forced her to retire five years ago. She could hardly make it up the stairs, poor thing. She was reluctant to go. She had been with me for fifty years. Loyal as the day is long. I installed her in the boarding house. It was the least I could do after her faithful service to me. Her room is on the second floor and there is an elevator. She writes to me regularly."

Dodo put her forefinger to her head. "Is she…you know?"

"If you are trying to ask me if she has all her marbles, I can assure you that she is still as sharp as a tack."

"As sharp as you Granny?"

The Dowager smashed her lips together and narrowed her crepe skinned eyes. "No one is as sharp as me," she said with a wicked grin.

"Then I think I want to go and see her. Do you suppose she will mind?"

"Mind?" said the Dowager pulling out her snuff tin. "It will make her day!"

Dodo and Charlie were racing down to Lancing in the Dorchester's sleek Bentley. She had called him first thing in the morning to invite him to join her. His voice told her he was encouraged that she had called so soon.

Currently, Charlie was admiring the Bentley's glossy wood interior from the passenger seat. They had the top down.

"Have you ever been to Lancing?" Dodo yelled over the rush of air.

"No. I've been to Brighton."

"Everybody's been to Brighton," she said with a grin. "Lancing is Brighton's poor cousin. Not fashionable at all but the same mild climate."

Dodo swerved as she careened round a corner and almost collided with another vehicle.

"I say, Dodo, you could slow down a tad." Charlie was now gripping the door handle so tightly his knuckles were white.

"Nonsense! I had bags of room," she declared with contempt.

The day was exceptionally fine, and many people seemed to have the same idea for a day at the coast.

"Do you think your father would mind if I had a go?" Charlie asked.

"Not at all. When we get to Lancing, we can swap."

"So, you have a wild idea that Colonel Winchester is somehow related to this soldier who died in the Anglo-Burmese war?"

Dodo smashed her hat further onto her head as the wind picked up. Charlie stared at her one hand that remained on the steering wheel.

"I suddenly remembered that Mr. Guthrie bumped into me as we went out on deck for the race before the murder was discovered. It was nothing really and must have slipped into my subconscious mind. So, you see, that doesn't give him time. He can't be the murderer. Mrs. Guthrie's times must be off and considering her guilty conscience it doesn't really surprise me. Guilt makes for unreliable witnesses. I left a message for the chief inspector early this morning but he was out." Dodo honked the horn at a slow car.

Charlie waved as the driver of the car made a rude gesture out the window. "I don't think that chap appreciates your need for speed," he said, laughing.

"If he wants to drive slowly, he should pull over and let me pass." Dodo laid on the horn again.

Charlie pulled his hat down over his eyes. Dodo ignored the implied message.

"So, we're back to square one, and I'm following a new lead. I want to try out that awful laugh on Mrs. Nibley and see if it's the same. And a lovely trip to the coast is always a treat."

As Dodo brought the car to the top of a hill, she passed the slow poke whose lips and arms were moving wildly. Charlie slunk down in his seat. At the crest of the hill, the Channel was laid out before them like a jade carpet.

"Marvelous!"

She pushed her foot onto the accelerator as they descended making her stomach jump delightfully. She glanced at Charlie whose brow was sharply furrowed.

As they neared the seafront, Dodo pulled over to the curb and caught the attention of a passing pedestrian. "I say, excuse me. Do you know where I can find the Silver Fox boarding house?"

The elderly pedestrian pointed left. "Third building on the right, miss."

"Thanks awfully."

The directions were good, and they soon found the place, white-wash gleaming, lots of windows and bright flowers in pots outside.

The lady at reception was barely tall enough to see over the wooden counter. She wore tiny round spectacles and grizzled gray hair in a tidy bun.

"Can I help you?" Her voice was high and squeaky, matching her appearance perfectly.

Her gaze lingered on Charlie.

"I hope so," said Dodo. "We have come to call upon Mrs. Nibley."

Cutting her eyes over to Dodo she asked, "Is she expecting you?"

"No. Will that pose a problem?"

The older lady's gaze swung back to Charlie, who was leaning lazily against her desk with a smile as warm as the sunshine outside.

"Not at all." She stepped around the counter. "She is out in the back garden. If you'll come with me."

They followed her through a dark, clean hallway that led to a well-maintained back door. As she pushed it open, sunlight flooded in and they stepped out into an Eden-type flower garden full of the heady scent of summer blooms. Small tables were dotted around the grassy area where elderly residents were enjoying the fresh air.

Everyone looked up as they came through, their interest peaked by handsome strangers. The landlady tottered over to a bent, old girl whose eyes squinted tight as they approached.

"Mrs. Nibley? These two young people have come to visit you."

Mrs. Nibley cast an appraising eye over the pair of them and Dodo felt quite naked. "Who did you say you are?" Her voice was throaty and cracked with age.

"I didn't," began Dodo. "My grandmother is the Dowager Dorchester."

"Dodo?" The suspicion slid off the old lady's face like ice from a sun-warmed window. "Why didn't you say so? Sit down. Sit down. And who is this handsome young man?"

The landlady, having ensured that all was well, walked away and they sat down at Mrs. Nibley's table.

She reached out a gnarled hand and placed it over Dodo's. "Oh, my dear! It has been years since I've seen you. You've changed so much and my eyes are weak. Please forgive my bad manners, m'lady."

"Do not worry yourself, Mrs. Nibley. Grandmother sends her best."

Mrs. Nibley's eyes, though hooded, were sharp and alert with intelligence. "How is she? I miss her terribly, but we write.

And she pays for this." She swept her arm around showing the garden.

"Grandmother is very fond of you. She is well. Sharp as ever."

Mrs. Nibley chuckled. "She never was a shrinking violet. I have some stories."

"I'm sure you do." Dodo felt an intense longing to hear those stories, but she had business to attend to before the old lady tired. The stories would have to wait.

Mrs. Nibley's eyes sparkled, drawing back a veil to her young soul. "Would you like some tea?"

"I would," said Charlie. "I'm parched after that harrowing drive."

Dodo shot him a look of scorn.

Mrs. Nibley rang a little bell that was sitting on the table between them.

A maid in a black dress and a dazzling white maid's bandeau opened the door they had come through and walked over to their table.

"Tea for three, please," Mrs. Nibley said.

As the girl left, Mrs. Nibley lowered her voice. "Not as good as my tea but not bad." She drew out a sharply pressed handkerchief and wiped her nose. "Now, why have you come to see this old lady?"

Dodo leaned her elbows on the table and steepled her fingers.

"I have a rather odd question that I'm hoping you can answer. You may have read about the murder of Lord Barchester at Ascot?"

"Oh yes. I read the newspaper every day. Shocking." She folded the handkerchief and slipped it back into her pocket.

"We were there." Dodo indicated Charlie with a nod. "We were actually guests in the same private box."

"You never were?" The old lady's eyes blinked with curiosity and Dodo laid out the tale again. "And how do you think I can help?" Her kind face was wrinkled like an apple left in the larder for too long.

"Lord Barchester and Colonel Winchester both served in Burma. I am trying to find if there is any connection between the two men. Granny told me that you had a sister whose son died in Burma."

"My sister's only child. Yes, that's right. Bit of a lad but she thought the army would sort him out. Instead it killed him. What of it?"

"Granny mentioned that he had a peculiar laugh."

Mrs. Nibley slapped her thigh. "That he did. He sounded like an elephant choking on a donkey."

Optimism swept through Dodo.

"Colonel Winchester has a similar laugh. If I mimic it, I am wondering if you could tell me if it is the same sound?"

Mrs. Nibley looked at her in shock that a lady would deign to make such a tawdry sound. "If you're sure. I could give it a try."

Pushing down any feelings of embarrassment, Dodo took a deep breath and mimicked the colonel's laugh. Every head in the garden turned towards her.

"That's it!" cried Mrs. Nibley. "It's a sound you never forget!"

"Do you think Colonel Winchester could be a relative of yours? It's a very distinctive sound."

Mrs. Nibley shook her head. "I wasn't blessed with any children myself, and my sister just had the one. Our brother died of scarlet fever when he was a boy. There are no other relatives."

Dodo tried not to let her disappointment show. "It was worth a try." She reached over to put her hand on the elderly lady's. "Now, tell me all those stories about Granny!"

Dodo and Charlie stayed until Mrs. Nibley's back started to bow and her lids began to droop.

"Give my love to the Dowager," she said as they shook hands goodbye.

"I will," promised Dodo with a kiss on her soft, lined cheek.

Back out on the street, Charlie looked along the promenade. "Since we're here, what do you say to a stroll along the pier?"

"Fabulous idea!" agreed Dodo, grabbing his hand.

It was a short walk to the windy pier, but the late afternoon was still warm. The briny smell and happy sounds of tourists created a festive feel.

"So, that seems like a dead end," Charlie said as they shared a pot of black, steaming winkles. They were a type of shellfish her mother frowned upon.

"Not necessarily," she contradicted, swallowing a winkle. "Is laughter hereditary?"

"Do *you* laugh like either of your parents?"

"It's not really something I have ever considered." Her lips twisted as she reflected. "I don't think so, but Didi and I sound similar."

"I sound nothing like my father," he said, proffering her another black winkle on the end of his fork.

"It's the only lead we have."

"Are you forgetting that Mrs. Nibley said there are no living relatives?" He dug the fork in, ready to spear another of the tiny black shells.

"What if there was an illegitimate child?" she asked.

"Wouldn't Mrs. Nibley know about it?" He poked the soft winkle out of its shell.

"Not necessarily. People kept such things very quiet back then."

A seagull perched close to them, eyeing their food. Dodo shooed him away.

"It's a long shot, but I think we need to go to Somerset House where they keep all the vital records. Births, deaths…that kind of thing. It couldn't hurt."

"If it means I get to be with you, I'm all for it." He planted a kiss on her forehead.

"I just need to satisfy my curiosity and see if there might be a connection between Colonel Winchester and this dead soldier."

"They're from different walks of life, surely," Charlie pointed out.

"But if he was adopted…" She bit her lower lip. "I just want to check into it."

At the end of the pier was a small merry-go-round, and Dodo had a sudden surge of childishness sweep through her. One thing she did like about Charlie was that she could be herself. So much of the time she spent creating and sustaining her sophisticated public image. Sometimes, a girl just needed to let her hair down.

Dragging an unenthusiastic Charlie, Dodo bought two tickets and they clambered onto a couple of white and gold carousel horses.

As the horses went up and down to the merry music, Dodo experienced a surge of fondness for Charlie. He must have noticed a change in her countenance as he tipped his head in question. In response, she clung to the brass pole with both hands, leaned as far back as possible and let her head fall back with abandon.

She would let him drive home.

Chapter 17

Somerset House, named after the Duke of Somerset who built the original structure in 1547, stood tall and proud. This edifice was now the home to the General Register Office where all the vital records of England and Wales were stored.

There was a pervasive staleness, reminiscent of a secondhand bookstore, which she supposed was logical since they were in the epicenter of old documents. Dodo and Charlie spent a good chunk of the morning looking through enormous registers of births in Northampton from sixty years before. On the one hand, the place filled Dodo with excitement that you could find proof of links to your ancestors, long dead, forming one great chain of humanity, and on the other, incredible sadness that a person's rich life was reduced to a series of dates for their birth, marriage, and death.

They were looking for a possible illegitimate birth to Mrs. Nibley's sister but after hours of searching they had found nothing.

At eleven o' clock, Dodo decided it was time to try a different line of attack.

After asking for directions to the military records department, they now approached the desk after a short wait in line. The fashionable young woman who worked there was unexpected, her appearance at odds with the musty records she worked with.

"How may I help you?"

"I am interested in war records, particularly the Anglo-Burma war of 1885."

A deep frown appeared on the young woman's face. "Oooh. That might be a problem. Was the person you are searching for an officer? Proper records weren't really kept until the Great War. We do have a room that contains regimental muster records, discharge and pension papers and miscellaneous journals, but it is not complete."

Her expression held a hint of pity. It was not encouraging, but after an unproductive morning, Dodo was determined to try.

"Can you take us to what you have?"

"Let me find someone. Wait here please." She disappeared into a room behind the desk whose upper walls were made of privacy glass.

After a few minutes, the efficient young woman returned with a diminutive man of indeterminate age. He had a fine, thin covering of light brown hair but his face was relatively unlined. He wore medium brown trousers, a white short sleeved shirt and a woolen vest in various brown hues. Utterly conventional.

"Follow me, please." His voice was similarly highly predictable.

Dodo and Charlie followed him down a corridor lined with mud-colored linoleum which deadened their footsteps. He stopped at a door where the top half was the same muted glass and pushed it open. The room was much bigger than Dodo expected and contained rows upon rows of shelves.

"Which wars are you particularly interested in?" the slight man asked.

"The Anglo-Burmese war of 1885," Dodo responded.

"Please, wait here." He pointed to a table in the middle of the room. "I will look for any records pertaining to that particular battle."

They did as they were bid. No one else was in the room, and they could hear their guide moving about and shifting boxes.

"Fancy working in a place like this," said Charlie, his mouth pulled down in a frown.

Dodo puckered her lips. "I thought the future Classics professor might find such a place as this rather thrilling."

"Touché!" Charlie responded. "However, I *read* the tomes, I don't babysit them. That's much more exciting."

At that moment, the clerk returned holding a large, dirty box. As he placed it on the table he said, "There's one more. I'll go and get it."

The lid had a thick layer of dust on it. No one had disturbed this treasure in some time.

Dodo looked down at it, her eyes wide with disgust.

"Here, let me wipe it down for you," said Charlie, gallantly brandishing his handkerchief and giving the lid a good clean. This sent tendrils of dust into the air and Dodo sneezed.

Lifting the box lid, they saw record books haphazardly piled in. "This will take a while," Dodo said with a wry grin.

"And he's bringing us another one." Charlie reminded her.

She took out the top book. It contained lists of supplies used by the troops in the war. No names as far as she could tell. She placed it on the table and moved on to the next book. This was more interesting as it was a diary of someone called Captain Wheeler. A brief glance told her it was not a personal journal but his record of different military strategies – their successes and failures. She added it to the book on the desk.

The clerk returned with a similar box. "Just put everything back in the boxes and leave them on the table when you're done."

Down and down the first box Dodo ploughed finding nothing of interest, the contents in untidy piles on the table like some bibliographic disaster.

She turned her attention to the second box whose lid Charlie had already cleaned. He was browsing through one of the military journals, legs outstretched.

Half-way down the second box, she removed a black book that listed deaths in the field. Now she was getting somewhere. The recorder was not skilled in the art of handwriting and she had to puzzle out the names which were written in sloping rows. She dragged her finger down the page looking for 'Haviland'.

Page after page of almost illegible script strained her eyes, and a dull throb began in her occipital bone. Ready to give up, her diligence was at last rewarded and her finger stopped sharp on the second to last page.

"Eureka!" she cried. "Found him. Matthew Haviland died April 14, 1887. By the look of it, lots of men died that day. An officer reported his death…" She hit the table and shocked Charlie into dropping the diary. "One Cuthbert Winchester, wounded."

Charlie's eyes crinkled at the edges. "You are very pretty when you've found a clue," he remarked. She punched him on the arm.

Turning to the last page she smacked the book.

"Wounded, Jeremy Barchester, age twenty-one."

Injected with enthusiasm by these finds, she fixed her eyes on Charlie as though she was a hunter and he a prize buck.

"*This* is the missing connection. Colonel Winchester, Lord Barchester and Matthew Haviland all served in the same theater of war in 1887. It is too much of a coincidence to be insignificant. I wonder if Lord Barchester recognized Colonel Winchester and was asking him about it the day of the race when Portia saw them talking?"

"So, they served together? It is a bit of leap to go from that to accusing the colonel of murder." Charlie closed the book he was reading.

"Portia said the colonel was shaking his head. Why deny you were there unless you have something to hide?"

"Are you seriously accusing someone in the Prime Minister's cabinet of murder? This information is hardly a smoking gun, though I admit it is suspicious. Dodo, we need to have more conclusive information before we start throwing serious accusations at such a high-profile man." He placed his elbows on the desk.

"You're right of course," she conceded, "but this *has* to mean something. There must be a correlation. We need to question the colonel."

Dodo absent-mindedly grabbed the next book in the box as her mind spun. It was a record of disciplinary action. She flicked through the pages thoughtlessly, her brain still wrestling with the previous discovery, until her eyes caught on a familiar name. Matthew Haviland.

"Here's his name again. Matthew Haviland. Written up for … inappropriate relations with a young Burmese girl. Golly, I think he compromised a native. Granny told me that some unethical things went on over there, but this is really villainous. If Haviland hadn't died, he would have been court martialed. His death saved his family from the shame of it."

"I think that is history best left undiscovered," Charlie said. "No family will benefit from knowing *this* truth after so many years have passed. Better to let sleeping dogs lie, I say."

"Mrs. Nibley is the only family left, as I understand it. And I agree that there is no need for her to learn of this. But I can't help feeling that there is some implication here." She closed the book and stood, hands on the back of the chair.

"You're the historian," she said after some thought. "Let's use your academic skills to learn all that we can about this war. I'll make a note of the dates and places in my notebook."

"The Cambridge college libraries are extensive," said Charlie. "Suddenly my expertise is valued." He winked at her.

"Imagine that," she purred.

Dodo began taking notes as Charlie put the redundant books back in the boxes.

"What a stroke of luck!" she remarked as she wrote. "I was beginning to think we were wasting our time."

Charlie dragged a hand across his face leaving a dusty, gray smudge.

Dodo took out her handkerchief and reached across the table to him. "Here, you've got a dirty mark." His hand lifted to brush the spot again as she skimmed his cheek with the cotton cloth. He grabbed her wrist and kissed it sending a pleasant tickle up her arm.

Once she had finished and the assortment of mis-matched books had been returned to their boxes, they left the airless building. The sun seemed excessively bright after the dingy reference room.

"It's only one o' clock," she said, looking at her watch. "I bet we can catch a train up to Cambridge and be there before three. What do you think?"

Charlie threw his arm around her shoulders. "I'm in."

***

Cambridge University Library was rather grand as libraries go. It looked like a palace with its dazzling white stone and Grecian arches.

When the lady librarian caught sight of Charlie, she beamed as though her face would crack.

"Mister Charles," she whispered, sounding like a proud mother. "What a pleasure to see you again. What are you doing here? Term doesn't start for weeks."

Dodo felt a welcome charge of affection surge through her as she saw Charlie through someone else's eyes. It couldn't be more obvious that Mister Charles was a favorite.

"Hello, Miss Bristwhistle. It's good to see you again." His smile told Dodo that the appreciation was mutual. "I need to do some research and where better than England's finest library?"

The plump librarian flushed with pride. "And who is this?" she asked, noticing Dodo and looking her up and down, appearing to appraise her worthiness.

Charlie clutched Dodo's hand and gently pulled her toward him. "Miss Bristwhistle, may I present Lady Dorothea Dorchester." He had stopped short of introducing her as his girl and Dodo wasn't sure how she felt about that fact.

"Well, aren't *you* the lucky one?" the spinster librarian crooned. "Mister Charles is one of the finest young men I have the privilege of knowing."

It felt odd to be incidental. Dodo was so used to being the center of attention, not because she sought it but because it happened—her title, her job as ambassador of fashion, her looks. Here, Charlie was foremost, and she found that she didn't begrudge him a bit. She knew firsthand how nice he was but there was something comforting about having his good character confirmed by a third party.

The librarian's smile became as warm as a freshly toasted crumpet. "Any friend of Mister Charles' is a friend of mine. Now, back to business. You said you needed to do some research?"

"Yes, the Anglo-Burmese war, 1885-1895," Charlie said.

"Whoo, that's some heavy reading," she said, throwing a questioning look at Dodo.

"Oh, I'm fascinated by it," Dodo confirmed with a devilish grin.

The librarian delivered her a look that said, *I suppose it takes all kinds.* "Follow me, dears."

There were few people about since term was over, just academicians in their black robes, as they followed the librarian to a huge, wooden cabinet of reference cards. Expertly, Miss Bristwhistle narrowed her search down to one area and within a few minutes had located the card she needed. "This way," she chirped, reminding Dodo of a friendly sparrow.

It was dark and stuffy among the stacks and Dodo wrinkled her nose.

Miss Bristwhistle pulled over a ladder, mounted and reached for the book she needed and handed it down to Charlie. "This whole section"—she waved at the books near the ladder—"is about that war. But this is by far the best book on the topic."

She dismounted and bestowed another matronly smile on Charlie. "Just leave them here when you're done. Someone will re-shelve it." She wagged her finger at him. "And don't leave without saying goodbye."

After promising that they would not slip away without a farewell, they sat together at the desk, arms pleasantly brushing, while Charlie flicked through the appendix.

"Here we are." He pointed to a tiny line of text. "This might have something. 'Lance Corporal Cuthbert Winchester'." He flicked to the page indicated and Dodo peered at a very grainy photograph of a group of men in uniform.

"Lance Corporal Winchester's unit was implicated in an incident of some infamy when several members raided a Burmese village without permission, defiling some of the daughters of the villagers and burning their huts. Later that night, the surviving male villagers wreaked revenge on the soldiers, slitting throats and stabbing them in the dark. Only Lance Corporal Winchester and one other soldier, Corporal Jeremy Barchester, survived the skirmish, though each was wounded in the attack and sent home to England after rudimentary on-site medical attention. This incident was a dark moment in the war, one the British Army regrets."

Charlie placed the book down. "Well, that's rather grisly."

"I know. But this proves that they did serve together. The colonel had to have known Lord Barchester. The hairs on my neck are quivering."

"Then why deny it?" asked Charlie. "Perhaps he was not as innocent of participation as this account seems to suggest?"

"What if Lord Barchester recognized the name 'Winchester' and asked him if he was the same Winchester that served as unit commander in 1887 in Burma? Something like this would tarnish his reputation and jeopardize his position in parliament. I imagine the colonel lied, claiming that his lordship was mistaken. But Felicity said Lord Barchester looked distracted after that conversation. It was forty years before, and people change considerably in that amount of time. Winchester is a common enough name, but together with his Christian name it would be incontrovertible. Lord Barchester was probably confused by the denial. Enough that he couldn't be one hundred percent sure. Enough that it bothered him."

"And you think the fact that he recognized Colonel Winchester as the man he served with got him killed?" asked Charlie.

"Think of what is at stake. Very few men will ever serve at that level of government. As a cabinet member, you are revered and earn a place in the history books."

"But if he *was* their leader and disapproved of his men's actions, why would it stain his character? He could counter any attack by claiming that the soldiers acted alone without authority, while he was asleep, and that they got what they deserved."

"But it would stir up controversy. The press would have a field day with it. And maybe the account we read is a pack of lies. You're an historian. How accurate is most history, honestly?"

"Well," Charlie began, "it is often written well after the event by someone who wasn't even present and who may or may not be lucky enough to interview people who actually were there. And of course, it is always slanted by the opinions and conclusions of the writer."

"So, by your own admission, it is very unreliable."

Charlie looked askance. "Yes."

"We need to talk to the colonel. If he was complicit, he would have a strong need to silence a witness."

Charlie's expression was suddenly serious. "I think you should share this information with the chief inspector and let *him* interview the colonel."

Dodo sighed. "I suppose you're right. Perhaps I can convince him to let us go along."

"You can always ask I suppose." He kissed her on the tip of her nose and closed the book. "Let's write down this book's reference information and call the chief inspector."

As they were leaving, they stopped by the librarian's desk as promised. Miss Bristwhistle moved around the desk, her countenance sunny, and stepped toward Charlie. She raised her arms then dropped them to her sides, plucking at her dress. Dodo suspected that the librarian really wanted to give Charlie a hug, but it was against all rules of decorum. Instead with the excess energy, she shifted from foot to foot as they said goodbye, smiling broadly.

"Where's the nearest telephone box?" Dodo asked him when they were back outside.

"There's a public one next to the Royal Arms. We can call and then eat dinner there."

She slid her arm through his. "Perfect."

It had been some time since Dodo had been to Cambridge. The sun was still high in the sky and glinted off the Cam. Perhaps they could go punting after dinner. It wouldn't get dark until around ten o' clock at this time of year.

Since it was the summer holidays, the streets were not crowded with the usual students or bikes and no one was using the public telephone. They squeezed into the bright red box together and Dodo dialed the operator.

Though it was late in the working day, the chief inspector was still in his office.

"Hello, Chief Inspector Blood? It's Dodo Dorchester."

"Lady Dorothea, how can I help you?" His voice was flat and lackluster.

"It is I that may be able to help you, Chief Inspector." She told him all that they had learned in Lancing, Somerset House, and the Cambridge University library.

By his rejuvenated tone, she could tell that her news had given him a needed shot in the arm. "By Jove, you've found out more than all my investigators!" he declared.

"Well, it was lucky that Granny knew something about it. That gave us a starting point. Do you think this is enough to interview the colonel again?"

"I do." She could hear papers rustling on his desk and the sound of a pen scratching notes.

She decided to risk refusal. "Might you consider bringing us along since we have been so helpful?"

There was a pause and Dodo knew he was biting the side of his cheek as he considered her question. "I might. Let me call and make an appointment. I'll telephone your home with a time for tomorrow, if possible."

She felt excitement percolate through her. They were getting close. She could feel it.

"Right you are! And thank you." She replaced the receiver.

She grinned at Charlie. "Tomorrow."

"Dash it! I can't do tomorrow," he said. "I forgot. I have a longstanding family obligation."

"Do you mind if I go?" she asked.

Charlie took a minute to answer, a kaleidoscope of emotions ranging over his face. He finally said, "Of course not! You've done so much of the leg work. You deserve to be there."

She kissed him quickly and he returned the kiss slowly and deliberately before they entered the pub to eat. His trust in her was comforting.

Do I deserve it?

Chapter 18

The colonel and Mrs. Winchester lived in a flat just across the bridge from Westminster. Dodo knew they also owned a house in Kent and had bought this to be close to the center of government while the colonel served with the Prime Minister.

As Dodo and Chief Inspector Blood met outside the apartment building, she found she could not comfortably meet his eye. This was the first time they had met in person since the disastrous debacle at his office. She had underestimated how much that incident had rattled her but seeing him now, she clasped her handbag tight and shifted her feet.

"Lovely weather for the time of year," she babbled, looking past his shoulder.

Oh my gosh! I'm an idiot.

She risked a peak and saw him laughing…at her!

"Surprisingly fine for June," he said with a grin as he pushed open the door to the apartment block, allowing her to enter the small lobby. Her cheeks were rosy from embarrassment as she brushed by him with her head down– not a feeling she was accustomed to.

The flat they needed was up two flights of stairs and she had no desire to be stuck in an elevator with him in her current state.

"Shall we take the stairs?" she asked, her foot already on the first step.

"If you like," the chief inspector replied, following behind.

Soon after the chief inspector knocked, a young maid in black and white uniform answered the door and let them in.

Dodo quickly stepped in to put some distance between herself and the inspector and was surprised by the small and narrow vestibule. There was just enough room for a coat stand. She had expected something more grandiose. As the maid took her jacket, Dodo noticed that the whole apartment was quite modest with, a sitting room on one side and a bedroom on the other.

Looking around she saw another door that led from the entryway that she assumed was a kitchen.

The maid motioned to the sitting room and then stepped behind them, announcing who the visitors were. They were expected.

Dodo glanced around the room as she crossed to sit on the red, damask sofa. Two matching armchairs were arranged around an ornamental fireplace, a dark, oak coffee table in front of them, and a large window looked across the river to the imposing palace of Westminster.

"Please sit down," said Mrs. Winchester in a tight voice. A portrait of her husband hung above the mantle. He was in full, regimental uniform and still had a full head of hair.

Both Winchesters occupied a chair, their faces stern.

"Good morning, sir. Mrs. Winchester. Thank you for making time to see me," the chief inspector began.

At that moment, the maid returned, laden with a tray bearing tea and biscuits.

Mrs. Winchester slid forward in her seat to pick up the teapot.

"Tea?"

Dodo was heavy with anticipation and had no appetite, but she nodded. The chief inspector did the same, thanking Mrs. Winchester, as he balanced the delicate, white china on his bony knee. "I have a meeting with the Prime minister shortly. I hope this won't take long?" snorted the colonel.

Both Winchesters eyed Dodo with undisguised suspicion. Her skin crawled.

"I took the liberty of inviting Lady Dorothea to join us as she has done some invaluable research. I hope you don't mind?"

The pair remained chilly but the chief inspector's praise caused a quiet shoot of happiness to poke through and quiet Dodo's uneasiness.

"I believe Lady Dorothea may have questions that relate to her work," he continued. "I have found her to be an intelligent and constructive interviewer in the past."

Dodo's satisfaction blossomed into a full-grown Gerber daisy.

Mrs. Winchester remained unconvinced, if her sour expression was any indication, but putting down her cup and saucer she began to speak.

"So, what questions do you have, chief inspector. My husband is a very busy man."

Colonel Winchester granted them a squashed smile that failed to reach his eyes.

"According to your testimony the day of the races and in your second interview, we understand that you served in Burma back in the 1880's," the chief inspector began.

"What on earth does that have to do with Lord Barchester's demise?" Mrs. Winchester's tone was indignant, her neck pulled high.

"Now, now Margaret," soothed the colonel. "Let them ask their questions."

Mrs. Winchester edged closer to the front of her armchair.

"That is correct, Chief Inspector. I did serve in Burma from 1887 to 1892 with a stint back home to recover from wounds received in battle."

The chief inspector placed his cup on the coffee table causing his overcoat to pop open, revealing a well-pressed, blue suit. "We are now aware that the late Lord Barchester served in the same area at the same time."

"Could be, could be," the colonel nodded and muttered, his tone non-committal.

"You don't remember him?"

Dodo admired the chief inspector's skill at weaving a careful noose for the colonel, all while keeping his face smooth of emotion.

The colonel's brows knit together to form one wooly 'v'. "Have you ever served in battle chief inspector?"

"Yes, in the Great War."

Dodo was surprised. This was something she did not know about him, but it would stand to reason given the chief inspector's age. She wondered what mental and physical scars he bore from his service.

The colonel stroked his immaculately clipped moustache, his eyes becoming intense as he said, "Then you know how chaotic things can be. Our theater of operation was a lot less civil than France, don't you know? Primitive, I might say. Soldiers were coming and going all the time due to injuries inflicted by the natives. They were not happy about losing their independence and took it out on our boys using guerilla tactics. No reverence for the rules of engagement. Shocking. Jeremy Barchester may have served in the same area as me briefly, but I have no recollection of it, I'm afraid."

The chief inspector smoothed the fabric of his trousers.

"Did Lord Barchester ask you about Burma the day of the royal race?"

Dodo could not believe that the chief inspector would not comment on the colonel's unlikely excuse, given what she had found in the records at Somerset House. Her grip on the teacup had tightened and she forced her fingers to relax in case she broke the delicate handle.

"Not really. He asked about the military and such, wondering if I had been there around the same time but I told him no, as I just said."

This time the chief inspector put down his pencil. "That is a surprise, Colonel, because we have uncovered a record that states that only two members of your company survived a counter raid by native villagers. You and Jeremy Barchester."

Finally! Dodo felt her shoulders stiffen as she awaited the colonel's response.

In contrast, the colonel's shoulders slumped almost imperceptibly. "As I explained, it was chaotic. There were several units assigned to that area. Perhaps Lord Barchester was with one of the others and since he was the sole survivor, they made a mistake and lumped him in with my men. I don't remember him." His gaze was cool and unwavering.

Chief Inspector Blood made a show of referring to his notebook for the next question, but Dodo was positive that it was a ruse. "You were injured in that raid, yes?"

"Yes." The colonel raised his trouser leg to reveal the nasty scar. "They were brutes. Slashing and stabbing with abandon. I lost a lot of blood and was taken for dead. It wasn't until a medic checked that they found a small pulse. I still have nightmares about that night." He wiped his mouth with the back of his hand.

With no pause the chief inspector asked, "And what about a Private called Matthew Haviland?"

Dodo snapped to attention as Mrs. Winchester choked on her tea, spilling a little onto the plush rug. "Oh, excuse me. How silly. Let me find Nora to wipe this up. If you will excuse me." She dashed from the room.

"Of course," said the chief inspector but Dodo noticed that he was watching her carefully as she left. He turned back to the colonel. "Matthew Haviland?"

The colonel's pallor was gray. "Doesn't ring a bell…who was he?" His eyebrows were now dancing around.

"The military report says that he got into trouble for taking advantage of a young native girl and was disciplined…by you."

The colonel's head reared back; lips pursed. "Haviland? Disciplined you say?" He tapped his chin with a finger. "Unfortunately, there were many infractions. Our boys sought revenge for all the raids. We tried to put a stop to it of course, but boys will be boys."

Dodo was horrified at his cavalier attitude toward the innocent young women who were at the mercy of his unruly troops. Disgust smoldered.

"So, you claim to have no recollection of this particular soldier?" The noose was nearing completion.

"You have to understand, we were disciplining whole units, Chief Inspector. One name would not stand out more than any other. And it was a long time ago. Forty years. Was he court martialed?"

The chief inspector moved his hat that sat on the coffee table. "He died before a trial could take place. During that counter-raid as it happens."

"Ah, well that would be why I don't remember him then. Had I been a witness at a trial, it would have made more of an impression on me." The colonel's bulky frame relaxed.

Mrs. Winchester now returned with the maid in tow and darting harried looks at her husband. The maid knelt down and scrubbed at the wet rug with a rag.

"Thank you, Nora," she said, dismissing the girl who could not be more than fifteen.

"So, we have you, Jeremy Barchester, and this Matthew Haviland all serving in the same war in the same area of that war. It feels implausible that you allege no memories of either man."

Bravo!

The colonel's lips narrowed. "If you say so, Chief Inspector."

The inspector took a biscuit from the tray. "It is not I that says so, sir. It is the military record that puts you all together."

The colonel shifted in his seat and pointed at the chief inspector. "Do you have any idea how many battles I have served in since then over the course of a twenty-year career? I cannot be expected to remember every man I served with."

"Perhaps not, but I am investigating a murder, and I cannot ignore the possibility that Lord Barchester may have recognized you."

Dodo thought the colonel might jump up but instead he threw his hands in the air. "So what if he did? How is it relevant? We were both injured. We were sent home to different military hospitals and then reassigned. It would have been a mere comma in the tomes of military history. I did not remember him and that is the end of it. It is not a time I care to relive." The colonel's cheeks were flushed and mottled.

Dodo felt as though she had been listening to an evasive political speech.

"Now, if there is nothing else, I have a meeting with the prime minister in fifteen minutes."

Dodo seized the moment.

"I believe you knew my grandfather, Lord Grenville Dorchester?"

The colonel sat back, the bluster over and looked past her in thought. "That was your grandfather? Yes, I believe our paths crossed once or twice."

"It was Granny that told me you knew him. Coincidentally, my grandparents' housekeeper was the aunt of Matthew Haviland. Small world."

Mrs. Winchester blanched. "Astonishing!" she murmured.

Dodo was busily formulating a plan, but it would need to be executed with stealth in a public place.

Not here.

"Do you have any more questions for the colonel, Lady Dorothea?" asked the chief inspector.

"That is all for now." Their reactions to her last statement had bolstered her resolve.

The chief inspector stood. Dodo followed suit.

"Thank you for your time, colonel. Mrs. Winchester." He retrieved his hat from the table.

Mrs. Winchester had withdrawn into herself since her return from the kitchen. Matthew Haviland's name had rattled her.

Why?

Nora showed them to the door.

In the hallway outside the flat, Chief Inspector Blood paused. "I should very much like to be a fly on their wall right now."

"Me too," Dodo agreed. "When you mentioned Haviland, it was as though Mrs. Winchester's world tilted."

The chief inspector pushed back his cuff to see the time. It was an old, gold watch with more than a few dents and bumps.

I wonder if those blemishes are from his time in the war?

She wanted to reach out and touch it. Instead she looked from the watch to his face and found him staring at her. Her throat constricted and his gaze bounced back to the watch.

"I think it's time to set a tail on both of them. If they are spooked, they may do something incriminating."

They walked outside into the summer sun with Westminster in the background. Trolley buses were whizzing across the bridge.

"May I offer a suggestion?" Dodo asked, holding onto her hat as a bus flew by.

A smile spread across his features transforming him from a police inspector to someone she would like to know better. "What did you have in mind?"

"I have an idea that I think will prompt a reaction from the colonel. Do you remember me telling you that he had a unique laugh? I know it sounds silly, but I can't help feeling that it was his laugh that sparked a memory in Lord Barchester that led to his death. If I had brought it up just now, it would have elicited a denial, but my idea is to use it as a shock technique in a public forum."

The chief inspector stepped back. "You really believe that the colonel is the killer? I'm not sure I'm ready to draw that conclusion. He was in the box the whole time – remember his injury makes going up and down the stairs difficult."

"Yes. Look, I know it seems logistically impossible, but at this point it makes a lot more sense than any of our other theories."

"And then there is the problem of motive," said the chief inspector. "As the colonel pointed out, what did it matter if Jeremy Barchester recognized him? He was the commanding officer and not involved in the unauthorized attack. This would not stain his reputation."

The chief inspector was repeating back to her all the problems she herself had found with her theory. But she was done with dead ends. It was time for action.

"But Charlie admitted that history is fallible. What if the record was inaccurate and the colonel *was* involved in the travesties that went on? Everyone else was dead—or so he thought. There was no one to contradict his version of events. Then suddenly, forty years later, up pops a ghost from the past who remembers what really happened…Someone who could destroy everything the colonel has worked for."

The chief inspector flipped off his hat and scratched his head. "That would certainly be a motive."

"Here's my plan. I would like to appear at a public event where the colonel is present and mimic that laugh to shock him and gauge his reaction. It is unusual and the colonel only did it once the day of the race. Granny has never heard it, so I believe it is something he takes pains to control tightly. The rest of the time he has a different laugh, more like a deep chortle. I think it was a mistake in the box that day."

The chief inspector looked across the bridge at Big Ben. "Prime Minister's Question Time this afternoon might work. I happen to know that some military exercises are up for approval and the PM wants to gain support. I'm sure he will have the colonel there as part of his entourage in his capacity as a military expert."

"How could I gain access to it?" asked Dodo.

"The Stranger's Gallery. Anyone is allowed to enter that gallery and witness government at work."

Dodo clapped her hands together. "Of course! I think my father took me there as a child. I remember thinking how naughty they all were."

"We could go together."

Dodo had been gazing at the swiftly flowing river Thames and jerked her eyes back to the chief inspector.

What was he suggesting?

"If you want?" he added, backpedaling his suggestion. His eyes were wary, as though he feared her rejection. "My credentials would ensure entrance…" His voice trailed off, his sudden vulnerability catching her off guard.

Yes!

"I think it's a marvelous idea, Chief Inspector," she replied, looking up into his brassy eyes. "What time should we meet?"

"Would you like to grab a bite to eat before?"

The chief inspector was full of surprises today. Feeling that she had the upper hand, she could not resist teasing him again.

She quirked a brow. "Are you asking me on a date?"

A slight rose color blossomed on his cheek. "N…n..no!" he stammered. "But if you think it inappropriate…"

The moment was slipping away and she was not about to let this opportunity pass without grabbing it.

"Inappropriate? Of course not. I was just joking. One has to eat, doesn't one, Chief Inspector? And I am ravenous." She was pretending more confidence than she felt.

His hand went nervously to his hat again.

"I know a little place on the other side of the bridge, off the main road," he said.

"Sounds perfect."

For a brief moment the hustle and bustle of the bridge traffic faded, and it was just the two of them.

Then Big Ben struck the hour.

"If you're ready?" His smile was sweet, and annoying butterflies started dancing the tango inside her.

They walked the short distance to the restaurant and were seated at a table for two.

For the first few minutes they fumbled through a clumsy conversation about food and drink preferences, looking everywhere but at each other. The butterflies progressed to the quickstep.

Relief poured over her like a spring shower when the food arrived, filling the awkwardness. She dug into her meal with uncharacteristic gusto.

The quickstep calmed to a waltz as she ate, and she determined to bring the conversation around to the case. Common ground.

"Did you ever get my message about Mr. Guthrie bumping into me when the body was discovered?"

"Not until I got back from interviewing him."

"I'm so sorry. It was such an insignificant thing that I didn't remember it until I was retelling the story for the umpteenth time and it jogged my memory."

"Much of police work is wasted time, to be honest," he said. "It comes with the territory." He gave her a tired smile that softened his rugged face and made her heart skitter. She slapped it into submission.

"Would you pass me the salt?" he asked.

As she lifted the glass salt container to pass it to him, their fingers touched, and a familiar jolt of energy crackled between them. They locked eyes briefly until he sprinkled the salt on his plate.

The butterflies were close to a breakdown.

Eyes still on his food, he spoke as if to his pie and chips. "Lady Dorothea, you once said that the walls between the classes would never come down." He raised his head, his coppery eyes catching the light like pennies in a wishing fountain. "Do you still believe that?"

The directness and honesty of his question dazed her momentarily, a knot forming in her throat. She swallowed hard before responding.

"I do." The fact made her incredibly sad. "Lord Barchester was having a devil of a time being accepted into the peerage," she continued. "The unspoken rules of high society are rigid and unforgiving. I fear that couples who try to revolt will struggle under a huge handicap that might spell the ruin of their relationship before it even really begins."

The chief inspector had stopped eating and was listening, head tipped as he considered her words.

"I think I agree with you." He nodded. "It could never work."

He looked back at his food.

What was he saying?

Suddenly her appetite fled but she forged on, pretending to enjoy the food.

When the chief inspector was done with his meal, he looked at his watch. "We'd better look sharpish." He beckoned the waiter over.

Dodo laid her knife and fork down with relief.

They hurried out onto the street and back into Westminster, Big Ben standing proud across the street and the Abbey just to the right. A sudden break in the traffic caused the chief inspector to grab for her hand and run. She followed, staring at their clasped palms, shocked by the intensity of emotion his touch generated.

As soon as they were across, he released her, his face unreadable. "Come on."

Are we ever going to address this unfathomable attraction?

They hurried to the gate, pushing past the queue, the inspector flashing his police credentials.

Once inside they rushed along the corridor, following the signs to the Stranger's Gallery. Finding a seat near the front, Dodo looked down onto the crowded chamber just as the Speaker opened the floor for Prime Minister's Question Time.

The Commons had been a chapel in its past, and the two opposing sides of government sat in what used to be the choir seats. The distance between the two sides was only the length of two swords and newcomers were always surprised by how small the Chamber was. The Stranger's Gallery was a balcony that looked down on the Chamber, that was about half full.

An MP jumped up to be recognized stating his name and the constituency he represented. Dodo scanned the seats in the Chamber of Commons for the colonel. She saw him seated on an upper bench. He did not see her.

The Speaker recognized the MP who asked a question about estate taxes. The question was very long, and Dodo soon lost the train of it. The Prime Minister stood to respond and as soon as he was done five more MP's shot to their feet to be heard. The one lucky enough to be recognized by the Speaker began another long question about widows and orphans. As his cadence began its descent, Dodo decided to capture the moment. Hiding behind someone's back she let out the loud, obnoxious laugh. Everyone in the Chamber and the Gallery looked in the direction of the sound. Dodo came back into view and locked eyes with the colonel. Terror was stamped on every feature.

Then things took an unexpected turn. The colonel slumped over in his seat.

Chapter 19

The chamber exploded with concern and the proceedings screeched to a halt as people crowded the colonel.

"Come on!" said the chief inspector. "Let's go!" He bolted from the Stranger's Gallery, down some stairs and along a narrow hallway to a door to the Commons. A guard lifted his arm to stop them, but the chief inspector flashed his badge. "I'm here on police business." He nodded toward Dodo. "She is with me."

The guard frowned. "Come on, man. Someone has collapsed."

At that moment two medics appeared. "Emergency inside!" cried one of the medics. The guard nodded, eyes wide and let them all pass.

The medics ran to the colonel who was surrounded by concerned members of Parliament. The colonel was out cold.

"Move aside!" commanded the first medic. The members moved back in the tight space and the ambulance man felt for a pulse.

"He's still alive," he gasped. "Let's get him on the stretcher."

As they moved him, the colonel began to come around but was disoriented. "Margaret," he groaned. "Margaret."

"Hush, hush," soothed Dodo. "She'll be here soon."

The medics rushed the colonel out of the Chamber, and Dodo and the chief inspector followed them to a small side door.

"We'll need to wait here for the ambulance," the second medic explained. "Do you know him?"

"I'm Chief Inspector Blood of Scotland Yard. I need to speak with the colonel on some business."

The medic jutted out his bottom lip and nodded.

As they stood holding the stretcher, the colonel began to stir again, his face restless. Without warning he started to speak—in someone else's voice! It shocked Dodo to the core.

"Margaret, I think they know."

The accent was all wrong, that of a working-class person. He was clearly delusional, ranting like a lunatic. "What shall we do?" he moaned.

Dodo could make no sense of his words and she looked at the chief inspector who was equally confused.

"Margaret," groaned the colonel, still in the stranger's voice.

"I think perhaps he has had a stroke that has damaged his mind," said Dodo, her mind whirling.

The colonel struggled to get up and the medics had trouble keeping the stretcher balanced. "Mum, I'll be back for tea before you know it." His complexion was becoming more ashen by the second.

Dodo felt the first stirrings of panic. Her actions had backfired horribly.

I hope the ambulance gets here soon.

"I'm sorry Mum, bringing shame on the family. I tried to make up for it." The colonel was beginning to thrash, and the chief inspector helped the medics with their burden.

"There, there." Dodo wiped his forehead with a handkerchief. "Help is on its way."

The little door opened revealing the ambulance driver and the colonel was placed inside the vehicle. Dodo and the chief inspector watched as the white ambulance lumbered out of the courtyard.

"That was odd," the chief inspector remarked. "I've never heard anything like it."

Dodo gripped her chin. "I recently read about a condition called multiple personality disorder. Perhaps the colonel suffers from a similar affliction?"

He stared at her as if she had just made it up. "What is that?"

"As I understand the matter, it's when the mind splits into different personalities. Two people in one body so to speak."

"Good grief! We'll have to mention this delirium to the doctors."

"I feel quite responsible," Dodo said as they began the short walk back over the bridge to the hospital. "I think my little experiment rather provoked the attack."

"When Lady Barchester was murdered you told me not to hold myself accountable," he said, slowing to face her and taking her by the wrist. "This is no time to punish yourself. You could not have known what would happen."

"Thank you. I needed to hear that," she responded.

When they arrived at the hospital a few moments later, he explained his title and that he needed information on a patient that had just arrived from Whitehall. They were directed down a corridor to the nurses' station where he again explained who he was. They were invited to sit on some hard chairs while the nurse went to find the doctor.

Shortly after, the double doors swung open to reveal Mrs. Winchester, her skin gray, her face a muddle of lines. When she caught sight of the chief inspector, she started like a rabbit who had spotted a fox.

"Chief Inspector?" Her voice was tremulous and weak.

"We happened to be there when it happened," he explained.

"What exactly *did* happen?" She laid an evil eye on him.

"We were watching Prime Minister's Question Time from the Stranger's Gallery," began Dodo, "and the colonel … collapsed."

"Collapsed?"

"Yes. Does he have a delicate heart?" Dodo asked.

"No. He's as strong as an ox. Did you…did you ambush him?" she accused.

Dodo glanced at the chief inspector before saying, "We were in the Stranger's Gallery." It was a partial truth. Her heart dangled on the edge of guilt.

The chief inspector rescued her. "Does your husband suffer from any mental illness, Mrs. Winchester?"

Her genuine expression of shock parted the emotional veil she had drawn down. "No! Whatever led you to ask that?"

"We were the first to attend to him," the chief inspector explained, "and he was ranting. His voice was …not his own."

Mrs. Winchester's hand flew to her mouth. Red splotches appeared on her wrinkled cheeks. "I have no idea what you are talking about. It must be the illness or something."

Nurses and orderlies were rushing by and Mrs. Winchester's eyes followed them as she asked in a tiny voice. "What ... did he say?"

"He was calling for you...and his mother," said Dodo.

Mrs. Winchester's eyes cut over to Dodo and in them a storm of fear was raging.

"Nothing else?" Mrs. Winchester's voice cracked and the hands that clutched her handbag were trembling.

"Not really. Nothing we could make sense of." The chief inspector did not reveal what had really happened and Dodo took the hint and remained silent on the matter.

Mrs. Winchester's shoulders relaxed. "Have you spoken to the doctor? Where is the colonel now?"

"We are still waiting to speak to him," said the chief inspector.

As if they had summoned the doctor, the wide double doors opened, and a tall man in a white coat pushed through, searching the room. Mrs. Winchester raised her hand, and the doctor strode toward her.

"Mrs. Winchester?"

"Yes."

"I'm Dr, Gourley. I'm afraid that your husband has suffered a heart attack."

Mrs. Winchester's legs buckled, and the chief inspector turned to catch her just in time. Scooping the unconscious woman into his arms, he placed her on a chair. Dodo fanned her face with her gloves while the doctor placed his stethoscope on the fainting woman's chest.

"I'm fine," she gasped, within seconds. "It was just a ... shock... that's all. Can I see him?"

"Of course, but you should wait—"

"Nonsense!" She wrestled to stand.

"If you insist." The doctor helped her up and leaning heavily on him, he guided the woman to her husband's room.

The chief inspector and Dodo were left alone again but before they could speak, a constable popped through the doors. "I waited until I saw the lady go. We followed her this afternoon as you asked sir, and she went to a travel agency where she bought two tickets for passage to America on the Queen Mary."

"Did she indeed?" said the chief inspector, looking along the corridor after the woman. "Well, done constable!" The younger man's chest expanded noticeably before he left the hospital waiting area.

"They're planning to run away—beyond the law. Innocent people don't do that," Dodo exclaimed.

They sat down together on the uncomfortable chairs.

The chief inspector ran his hands down his face. "Let's review the whole crime casting the colonel and Mrs. Winchester in the role of the villains."

"Alright," said Dodo. "Charlie and I arrived after most of the other guests but before the Guthries. The room was divided between the young people and the older couples." She could almost smell the pastries again.

"Right," continued the chief inspector. "Then the Guthries arrived and the races began. At some point the colonel sat with the young people, as politicians do, and let out a very unusual laugh."

Mrs. Winchester's bark came sharply back to Dodo's mind. "I remember that his wife spoke up right then and told him to leave the young people to themselves." At the time Dodo had thought his wife's tone exasperated, but what if she was actually fearful? Granny said she had only heard the colonel guffaw, which meant he went to great lengths to conceal his true laugh. Why?

"If it was a laugh he was usually careful to hide, his wife would be angry at him for slipping up that day." *And it means she was familiar with the laugh and the danger it represented. Which is what exactly?*

Dodo looked over the chief inspector's shoulder, thinking. "Lord Barchester must have recognized the laugh from the past. It stirred up memories and he asked Colonel Winchester if he was the same Winchester who had served in the army in Burma in the 1880's. The colonel vehemently denied the claim. Portia saw him shaking his head firmly. But the question worried the colonel, because he *was* that Winchester." She clapped her hands together.

"Wouldn't Lord Barchester have recognized him?" asked the chief inspector.

"Forty years is a long time and people change, especially if they have done so on purpose. A change of hair, a little weight…" Dodo narrowed her eyes, remembering the colonel's bald head, thick whiskers and heavy frame. "But laughs don't change with age."

"Indeed," said the chief inspector. "Imagine if Winchester had done something illegal in the past, something that was not recorded in the military record but was known to Lord Barchester. Perhaps the colonel was not an innocent in the raids. Perhaps he turned a blind eye or even encouraged it. That laugh brought the long-buried memory to the surface and bothered Lord Barchester's conscience."

The pieces of the puzzle were finally falling into place. Just a few holes left.

"Felicity and Portia did notice that Lord Barchester was distracted," said Dodo.

A sudden flashback of the Winchesters in a tête à tête seemed to validate her theory. "The colonel informs his wife that Lord Barchester has remembered him and they hurriedly devise a plan to save his career. They must separate him from the group. They write a vague note suggesting a clandestine rendezvous. They have probably heard rumors of his penchant for dallying."

Dodo's hand flew to her neck. "Oh, my word! We are suggesting that Mrs. Winchester lured Lord Barchester, are we not? That she was an accomplice," cried Dodo.

"I suppose we are," the chief inspector nodded. "It accounts for the colonel's gammy leg and the difficulty of the stairs. He could have shielded the door as Mrs. Winchester left so that no one saw her."

"And she must have removed that very distinctive pink hat," added Dodo. "I remember that it was sitting at an odd angle when you questioned her."

The chief inspector turned his own hat round and around in his hands. "With the colonel covering for her, she could have slipped out *before* Lord Barchester, which is why Felicity didn't notice her as she went down the stairs to the ladies'."

"Then Mrs. Winchester waited for Lord Barchester under the stands, plunging the knife into the poor man before he realized what was happening," continued Dodo, slapping her knee with excitement.

"It was very risky, but they were desperate," concluded the chief inspector. "She stabbed him quickly, wiped the blade clean and slipped it back into her handbag. When she returned, it would have been easy to place the knife back into the beef roast."

Dodo's mind reeled.

"It would also mean that it was *she* who killed poor Lady Barchester," said the chief inspector.

Dodo let out a heavy sigh. "She is the very devil!"

"They couldn't take the risk that Lord Barchester would mention knowing that laugh from his days in Burma to his wife," continued the chief inspector. "They had to get rid of her. Mrs. Winchester knew that Lady Barchester was feeling adrift in society and she would have had no suspicions of a member of government's wife whom she had met the day before. Mrs. Winchester was probably offering sympathy—"

"—which given that *she* caused the loss is truly diabolical." Dodo was warming to the theory. "She could easily slip the poison into her tea when her back was turned."

"It is a theory that satisfies everything," stated the chief inspector.

Dodo stopped short. "Yes, but we have no proof." She stood and paced along the hospital corridor deep in thought. Something was still niggling at her.

Why was the laugh so important that it caused the colonel so much stress that he had a cardiac arrest? What had he done that was so wicked that they needed to cover it up? And how did two men who were in service together have the same unusual laugh? One an officer and one a private?"

Dodo slapped her hands together.

"What if the colonel isn't the colonel?"

The chief inspector sat down with a thump and shook his head. "What on earth do you mean?"

Dodo came to stand in front of him.

"What if the colonel is actually Private Haviland who was scheduled for court-martial for rape in 1887?"

Chapter 20

The chief inspector jumped up out of his seat. "What on earth do you mean?"

Dodo held her palms up as she explained her reasoning. "What if Matthew Haviland switched identities with then Second Lieutenant Winchester? It would explain the fact that they have the same laugh. And make more sense of the alter-ego we just witnessed."

He shook his head with disbelief. "But how would such a thing be possible?"

"The colonel told us himself that the war in Burma was in turmoil and somewhat lawless. Add to that the fact that everyone in the unit was killed, or so he thought, and that Haviland was facing a court martial. As the only survivor, it presented him with the perfect opportunity to reinvent himself." Dodo felt her brain firing on all pistons. "We know he was wounded. If he quickly changed his clothes and identification papers with the dead lieutenant and then waited to be rescued, when they asked his name, he would just groan 'Winchester' and his papers would confirm it."

The chief inspector scratched his chin. "What about his voice, his manners?"

"He had been under the command of Winchester and would know his voice and would have been highly motivated to act the part. He was sent away to be treated in England and he believed none of his unit had survived. After convalescing he probably put on some weight, changed his appearance and voilà, the new Winchester."

"I can see a whole host of problems with this scenario." The chief inspector sighed.

Dodo ignored his doubts and pressed on. "Mrs. Nibley's sister received official notification of her son's death. He obviously never made contact with her again. It was too risky, and things were going well. Plus, he served a further eighteen years in the army as Cuthbert Winchester, long enough for his appearance to change naturally and for any relatives to die out."

The chief inspector pulled his ear. "I still think it's a long shot."

But Dodo could tell that he was coming around to the idea.

"You must admit, it does fill in some of the gaps. What we need is some hard evidence. What if we could find a photograph of the whole battalion?" Dodo asked.

"And how would you go about that?" replied Chief Inspector Blood.

"I can make another visit to Somerset House. I wasn't looking for photographs last time, but I did find a grainy one in a book in Cambridge. Perhaps there are more?"

The chief inspector gripped his hat. "We would need to do it as soon as possible."

Dodo grabbed her clutch purse. "I'll pop there tomorrow morning. Is that soon enough?"

"Perfect!" The chief inspector lifted his arms as if to embrace her, and quickly dropped them.

She raised her brows in surprise and was astonished by an acute longing that washed over her, followed immediately by a residue of remorse. What did all these feelings say about her standing with regard to Charlie?

He buttoned his suit jacket. "And I will alert the ports and stations to bar entrance to Mrs. Winchester in case she tries to do a runner."

***

After much soul searching, Dodo had called Charlie with the latest update. He was more than eager to help. They now sat in the familiar room at Somerset House with the old record boxes spewing their contents again. This time they concentrated their search on photographs. Charlie had found a hardbound book with a history of the battle and the same grainy shot they had seen in the Cambridge library. Dodo opened her bag and withdrew a magnifying glass.

Charlie threw back his head and laughed with no restraint.

"What's so funny?" she asked, slightly annoyed.

"It's such a stereotype of a 'gumshoe'. You'll be pulling out a deerstalker next."

Dodo rolled her eyes. "Let's keep focused on the job at hand, shall we?"

Charlie sucked in his cheeks to stop himself from snickering as Dodo leaned over the picture with the glass. There were about fifty men, all in uniform and all staidly staring at the camera. Quite frankly, many of them looked just the same—helmeted young soldiers, stern expressions, set jaws. The picture was too small to be definitive.

She smacked the magnifying glass on the table. "Oh, you have a look. I can't honestly tell."

Charlie peered for several minutes before shaking his head.

"We need a clearer picture. Let's keep looking."

Dodo tipped the first box upside down, the last remaining items crashing onto the table- top. She looked inside the empty box to ensure that everything had fallen out, when she found a piece of paper stuck to the bottom. Pulling it free, she saw that it was not a piece of paper but the backside of a photograph that had browned around the edges. The picture showed five men poised as if for battle. With fewer subjects, the image was closer and less blurry. She took up the magnifying glass again. One of the men was clearly an officer, and the other four appeared to be enlisted men. She peered at the officer. He was fair with light eyes and a soft chin. Then she analyzed each of the regular soldiers. Two of them had dark complexions and dark eyes. The other two were fair, one was a little chubby and shorter than the other men, but the last man was similar in height and build to the officer.

"Take a look. What do you think?" She was pouting and Charlie planted a kiss on her ready lips. She frowned. "This is not the time, Charlie."

"You're right." He grinned in that cheeky way he had. "Not the time at all."

She swatted his shoulder as he took up the picture.

His mouth twisted to the side. "It just looks like a group of men, some dark and some fair. I don't see any particular resemblance."

"Me neither." She blew a puff of air up through her hair. "Dash it!"

Charlie stretched out in his chair like a cat waking up from a nap. "But the Winchester's don't need to know that."

Dodo swung her head to look at him. "What do you mean?"

"Though I am a reformed man, I did learn a thing or two from gambling," he said, brushing his hand along her lower lip affectionately. "We could run a bluff."

"You mean, pretend that the photograph is conclusive, to draw out a confession."

"Exactly."

"Oh, Charlie!" she cried, kissing him on the cheek. "You are brilliant."

"So they tell me," he said with a charming smile.

***

"Chief Inspector?" Dodo telephoned as soon as they found a phone box. Her last encounter with the chief inspector had disoriented her, flaming the feelings she had attempted to douse. The 'date' had definitely crossed some kind of social line.

The outing to Somerset House with Charlie had confused her even more. He was so sweet, so right for her. This war of affections was exhausting, and she was glad to have the crime solving as a way to avoid having to unpack her feelings. However, the necessity of calling the chief inspector highlighted her cowardice. She was glad that Charlie opted to wait outside.

"Lady Dorothea. What can I do for you?"

Was it her imagination or was his tone more tender?

How do I feel about that?

"Charlie and I returned to the military records room at Somerset House, and we may have found something."

"Is it proof of our suspicions?"

"Unfortunately, not. It's a photograph of a group of soldiers with no names written on the back to indicate who they are, but Charlie came up with a brilliant scheme. Are you a poker player, Chief Inspector?"

"What has poker got to do with anything?"

It crossed her mind that she actually knew very little about the chief inspector as a man. "Do you?"

"Occasionally. I prefer watching football with what little spare time I have."

She scrunched her nose, glad that he could not see.

"Well, as you know, a major part of poker is bluffing," and she explained their idea.

"That is rather ingenious. At this point I think it is a reasonable gamble. We need to push them into making a mistake. I say we give it a try. I'll take responsibility if it backfires."

***

Dodo and Charlie had taken a taxi and were now in the hospital, the photograph in her handbag, awaiting the chief inspector. Her nerves were more about being in the same room with Charlie and the chief inspector than about the ruse they were about to run.

As Chief Inspector Blood breezed through the doors in his shabby raincoat, Dodo was aware of the feelings she was trying to suppress, poking out their heads. She took Charlie's hand.

The chief inspector reported that his own investigators had looked into the colonel's family history. They had discovered that he was an only child of only children and that Winchester's parents had died in a flu epidemic before the Anglo-Burmese War. He had been born abroad and had attended several foreign boarding schools from the age of eight. All factors that would make him a vulnerable candidate for identity theft. After the infamous raid in Burma, he had been promoted and gone on to a distinguished career in the army.

"Mrs. Winchester has been here for the last half an hour according to my constable," he told them. "I have cleared our interview with the colonel's doctor. He has made a decent recovery and is lucid. Let's go."

They walked past the nurses' station and into a private room with a picturesque view of the river. Mrs. Winchester was talking in a low, serious tone and started as they entered. Her face clouded and she walked over to the door.

"Really! Is nothing sacred?" she cried. "My husband has suffered a serious illness and you offer no compassion but instead come here to badger him." Stress was radiating from her like light from an electric bulb.

"It's alright, Margaret," the colonel croaked in his usual voice. "We have nothing to hide."

The chief inspector went to stand by the colonel's head.

"We have some further questions," he began. "I must begin with asking why you were so alarmed when Lady Dorothea mimicked your laugh in the House of Commons?"

The colonel's eyes darted left and right and his mutton chops rose and fell. "I don't know what you are talking about. I heard no laugh. I was struck with a tight pain in my chest that winded me. The next thing I knew I was in the hospital."

"If you insist, sir."

Chief Inspector Blood withdrew his notebook, but Dodo suspected it was merely a prop. "We have learned that you and Mrs. Winchester have booked passage on the Queen Mary for America. It seems a strange time for a holiday considering the work you are involved with in government."

Mrs. Winchester lifted both arms as though she was exasperated with a small child. "Not at all! I thought Cuthbert deserved a holiday. Working in government is extremely stressful and I felt that he needed a rest."

The chief inspector narrowed his eyes.

"I'd like to go back to your service in Burma, with Lord Barchester," he said, ignoring his wife's response.

The colonel struggled to sit up more against his pillows. "I told you, I don't remember serving with him."

"That *is* what you told me, sir but we now have reason to believe otherwise."

Dodo witnessed a hasty look of panic pass between the husband and wife.

"Private Matthew Haviland was scheduled to be court martialed for compromising a young native girl. Unfortunately, he was killed before he could be brought to justice by the court system. At least, that is what we were led to believe. Lady Dorothea undertook some more research and found an old photograph of the regiment, stuck in the bottom of a dusty box, in a dingy room, deep in Somerset House. She noticed a strong resemblance between Private Haviland and his commanding officer, Cuthbert Winchester." The chief inspector walked to the end of the bed, pulling the photograph from his pocket. Dodo noticed his fingers crossed at his side. "I put it to you, that you, sir, are not Colonel Winchester but one Matthew Haviland—"

"Margaret, save yourself!" screamed the sick, old man in the bed.

Like lightning, Mrs. Winchester flew out the door and down the corridor with the chief inspector, Dodo, and Charlie hot on her heels. Incredibly fast for someone her age, she ran through the door to the stairs.

"I'll take the elevator to the ground floor," shouted Charlie, peeling off and running toward the elevator. Dodo hesitated, unsure of who to follow, until Chief Inspector Blood ran to the stairwell and looking up, indicated that he could see the feet of Mrs. Winchester.

Decision made.

They hurried up the stairs.

There were several more floors and the older lady showed no sign that she was slowing down. Near the top, Dodo saw light as a door opened and the fugitive ran onto the roof. When they reached the door, the chief inspector put his hand up to stop Dodo.

"She may be on the other side with a weapon. We know what she is capable of, Lady Dorothea. Let's take it slow." He pushed gently on the door and peered through the gap. He opened it farther and beckoned Dodo to follow.

The sun was bright after the dim stairwell, and Dodo was momentarily blinded as they made their way carefully across the roof, hiding behind chimney stacks and vents as they carefully searched for the desperate woman.

Without warning, Mrs. Winchester rushed them from behind, a knife in her hand, and the chief inspector yanked Dodo into a small enclosure with a door, slamming it shut. There was really only space for one person, causing them to be crushed together, Dodo's head fitting just under the chief inspector's chin.

Her heart slammed against her ribs.

Mrs. Winchester was battering the door with her fist, screaming, as the chief inspector held the handle tight. Dodo was shoved so close to the chief inspector that she could feel his erratic heartbeat against her as his ragged breath kissed her forehead. In this confusion, her emotions exploded in a chaos of feelings that had nothing to do with the crazed woman on the other side of the door.

Now I see fireworks! This is madness!

"Are you alright?" he whispered.

She nodded and his chin caught her hat, knocking it askew.

"You have ruined everything!" screamed Mrs. Winchester. "We are people of consequence, respected. The Prime Minister of England depends on my husband's experience and wisdom. How dare you interfere!"

The chief inspector moved his head down slightly in the cramped space, causing his stubble to brush her lips. Her insides caught fire.

"Sorry," he said trying to shift his position.

There was no light in the cupboard, for which Dodo was grateful as she could feel the heat rising from her burning cheeks. She took a deep breath, trying to calm her nerves and steady her disobedient heart.

"Cuthbert confessed everything to me," screamed Mrs. Winchester. "Years ago. He had been talking in his sleep. His accent and voice were so different. I asked him about it, and he told me the whole story. I'm a loyal wife and it was long in the past. He had made amends through his conduct since that time. I forgave him and together we became a powerhouse. I am the woman behind the man. He would be nothing without me."

She had stopped rattling the door handle and Dodo could hear her pacing outside the cupboard door.

"Then Cuthbert spoiled everything that day at the races with that stupid laugh. The only vestige of his former self. We were always *so* careful. But then again, what were the chances that it would mean anything to anyone there that day?"

A thud on the door told Dodo that Mrs. Winchester was stabbing at the door with the knife. She could feel the chief inspector tense, his chin slide across her hair as he gripped the handle tighter, sending ripples of warmth down her spine.

She buried the desire to scream.

"I had no idea who Jeremy Barchester was. No idea that he had served with Cuthbert all those years ago. Cuthbert certainly did not recognize him. Of all the people in England, it had to be he who was invited as a guest that day! The Devil's own luck!" Her fist pounded the door again.

"It touched a memory, but the memory was of a fellow soldier…Matthew Haviland. Not the young Lieutenant Winchester. Cuthbert denied it, of course, but I could tell that Lord Barchester was unsettled. He was searching his memory for the truth. That's when I knew we had to get rid of him."

A full confession. It was everything they needed.

Dodo heard Margaret Winchester's footsteps move away.

The chief inspector moved his other hand, accidentally grazing her cheek. Dodo's heart leapt like a flame on dry wood.

Why did that never happen with Charlie?

"Did I scratch you?" His voice was laced with softness and she experienced a sudden, insane impulse to kiss him.

Do I really care for him or is it simply a byproduct of this bizarre and dangerous situation?

She was scared. And not because a mentally unhinged woman was trying to kill her.

Dodo looked up to see a tiny sliver of light catch his reddish-brown irises looking down at her with undisguised tenderness. The air became thick as fog between them. Attraction surging in the impossibly cramped quarters. It took all her will power not to sink into him.

"It was obvious that Cuthbert couldn't do it with his bad leg. It *had* to be me, and it had to be swift. Violet Guthrie had told us about Lord Barchester's reputation. Disgusting! Unworthy! I knew he would not be able to resist the idea of a romantic liaison."

I was right!

"What about Lady Barchester? Why did *she* have to die?" The inspector's voice rumbled pleasantly through Dodo's ribcage.

"I couldn't take the risk. What if he told his wife of his suspicions? She had to be silenced."

Dodo felt dizzy, her pulse pounding in her ears like a steam engine, drowning out most of the noise outside.

"Stop!" Charlie's voice sliced through Dodo's internal turmoil like a blade. "Stop! Mrs. Winchester, you are surrounded by the police."

Dodo's knees sank.

As the chief inspector turned the handle, she heard rapid footsteps.

"No!" Charlie's cry hung in the air.

As they fell out of the cupboard, she saw Charlie at the roof's edge, hands in his hair. Dodo ran to his side and looked down, covering her mouth with horror.

Mrs. Winchester was no longer a threat to anyone.

Chapter 21

Charlie wrapped her in a comforting embrace, and she buried her face in his shoulder, but the contrast to how the chief inspector's nearness had made her feel could no longer be ignored—or acknowledged.

Chief Inspector Blood had been all business after they exploded from the cupboard and had run around organizing his policemen. While *her* natural instinct was to examine every last detail of what had just happened and the undeniable mutual explosion of feelings. But there was no time for that now.

Instead, Dodo and Charlie stood together on the roof, an island in a sea of blue uniforms running hither and thither, doing what was necessary. Charlie pulled her head onto his shoulder. The adrenalin and deluge of feelings were slowly draining out of her system, causing her to shake violently.

They waited an hour, drinking weak hospital tea, until the chief inspector found them and asked them to follow him to the colonel's room. The colonel's face was gray and haggard. He had aged twenty years in the last sixty minutes. His eyes briefly darted to the chief inspector as they entered but returned to the coverlet on his bed, his brows pinched.

"It is over. Your wife confessed to many things," began the chief inspector. "Filled in most of the gaps. You will be arrested as her accomplice."

The colonel's lips began to move.

"We looked uncannily alike, Winchester and I. People remarked on it. But we were from different sides of the tracks. Completely. My mother and father were in service." The accent was the old one, not the one he had developed for survival.

"He had mentioned that he had no living relatives, and I also knew that we were both only children.

"One night, the other privates and I had been drinking too much, and in a show of false bravado someone suggested that we go and show the natives what for. It was stupid and we were hopelessly drunk. As we entered the village, a beautiful young woman was bringing water back for her family and the devil entered me and I accosted her.

"I immediately felt sick at what I had done, and we hurried back to base before our misdeeds were discovered. But evil actions often lead to worse consequences. Winchester could see that we were somber and questioned us until one of the privates broke and told him everything. He was furious and drew up paperwork for a court-martial. My career in the army was over before it had started.

"We went to our tents, but I could not sleep. I had disgraced my family. It would crush my mother."

The colonel's fingers picked at the covers.

"In the early hours of the morning, the men of the whole village ambushed our tents, cutting and thrashing everything in sight in revenge, screaming that it was for the honor of their daughter.

"Winchester was asleep in his cot and was one of the first to be killed. He never knew what hit him. I was slashed and left for dead and before I fainted from loss of blood, I saw that everyone else had been killed. I had no idea there was another survivor.

"When I regained consciousness, I crawled to Winchester's tent. I saw instantly how things were and thinking I was the only one who survived, I grabbed my chance. I stripped off my uniform and grappled with Winchester's and swapped them, along with our identification papers, then I dragged his body to where the others lay, with my papers, and crawled back to lay down in his cot to await rescue." Hot tears rolled down the colonel's leathery cheeks.

"I pretended to be delirious so that I did not have to speak and was shipped back to England--as an officer. I practiced Winchester's voice and accent for the next three months while I recuperated. I kept waiting for someone to call me a fraud and oust me, but it never happened.

"I let my sideburns grow longer and styled my hair differently, gaining a few pounds deliberately."

Just as I thought.

He lifted his head, eyes squinting as if life was too bright...or too painful. "When it was time to return to the front, I asked for a completely different assignment, citing trauma if I were sent back to the area where I had been injured.

"I was very careful never to laugh out of control. It was the only distinguishing factor left of Matthew Haviland. And he was dead."

"I felt terrible for my poor mother, but it could not be helped. I worked hard and rose through the ranks on my own merits until I was a respected colonel.

"Sometimes I would pinch myself that little Mattie Haviland from Northampton was on the Prime Minister's cabinet, but I couldn't tell anyone…except Margaret." The broken old man wept.

The colonel's tears did not touch her. Dodo felt no pity for the man who had not only raped an innocent girl but killed two people to cover it up.

Dodo and Charlie left the room.

***

It was four in the morning by the time they walked out of the hospital and Charlie led Dodo to a bench on the riverbank to watch the sun rise. The smell of the dank water wafted through the air as the early birds began to sing, breaking the still of dawn.

A tight band was wrapped around Dodo's heart and dread filled her veins. Things had become crystal clear in the closet. The time had come to tell Charlie the truth.

"Charlie," she began.

"Yes." He kissed the top of her head as he held her close under his arm.

"I have really enjoyed these last couple of weeks together…" She felt him stiffen. "I have always valued your friendship…"

Charlie pulled away slightly so that he could look at her face, but she kept her eyes trained on the water flowing by.

She pushed on. "But I do not think it is fair of me to keep seeing you."

She risked a quick look at him and wished she had not. He looked like a little boy whose dog had been killed by a car. It ripped at her heart.

"Charlie, you deserve more than I can give you."

There she had said it.

There were no contradictions, no reprimands, just a chilling silence as he removed his arm from around her and hung his head in his hands.

For once she could not bear the silence. "You are every girl's dream but I just…I do not feel as I should …as you deserve. I kept telling myself to give it time, but it didn't help… I'm so sorry."

"We can keep trying," he moaned. "I want to keep trying."

"It's just not there, Charlie."

"Is it because of him?" Charlie's voice was flat, resigned, not laced with venom as she deserved.

"Him?" Though she knew exactly who he meant. "I don't know."

"It is. It's him, isn't it? I knew it that day we were in his office. You tried to deny it, but I knew."

This was no time for denials.

"Does he know?" asked Charlie.

"No!"

"What will you do?"

"Nothing. It would never work." A single tear tracked down her face. "Cannot work. An earl's daughter and a policeman." Her laugh was hollow. "I need to go away. Clear my head. Escape." She shook her hair back and wiped her tears. "I have cousins in the West Country. I think I shall go there. Creep away like a coward."

Charlie turned in his seat, kissed her forehead, then rose and walked slowly away, swallowed by the early morning mist.

And Dodo sat, head bowed, shoulders shaking, tears rolling down her cheeks, as the City began to awaken around her.

The End

I hope you enjoyed this cozy mystery, *Murder at the Races*, and love Dodo as much as I do.

Book 4, *Murder on the Moors*, is available now on Amazon. https://amzn.to/3aGEHi2

"A disastrous romance finds Dodo anxious to get out of town. Deciding to visit some cousins in Dartmoor, she looks forward to a week of healing and relaxation in the Devonshire countryside. But her plans are derailed when one of the guests does not return from a hike on the moors. An extensive search leads to the sad discovery of a body. All clues point to the insufferable Rupert Adley III. But Dodo is unconvinced. Can she discover the real murderer?"

Interested in a free prequel to this series? Go to https://dl.bookfunnel.com/997vvive24 to download *Mystery at the Derby*.

Book one of the series, *Murder at Farrington Hall* is available for $.99 on Amazon. https://amzn.to/31WujyS

"Dodo is invited to a weekend party at Farrington Hall. She and her sister are plunged into sleuthing when a murder occurs. Can she solve the crime before Scotland Yard's finest?"

Book two of the series, *Murder is Fashionable* is available for $1.99 on Amazon. https://amzn.to/2HBshwT

"Stylish Dodo Dorchester is a well-known patron of fashion. Hired by the famous Renee Dubois to support her line of French designs, she travels between Paris and London frequently. Arriving for the showing of the Spring 1923 collection, Dodo is thrust into her role as an amateur detective when one of the fashion models is murdered. Working under the radar of the French DCJP Inspector Roget, she follows clues to solve the crime. Will the murderer prove to be the man she has fallen for?"

For more information about the series go to my website at www.annsuttonauthor.com and subscribe to my newsletter.

You can also follow me on Facebook at: https://www.facebook.com/annsuttonauthor

About the Author

Agatha Christie plunged me into the fabulous world of reading when I was 10. I was never the same. I read every one of her books I could lay my hands on. Mysteries remain my favorite genre to this day - so it was only natural that I would eventually write my own.

Born and raised in England, writing fiction about my homeland keeps me connected.

After finishing my degree in French and Education and raising my family, writing has become a favorite hobby.

I hope that Dame Agatha would enjoy Dodo Dorchester at much as I do.

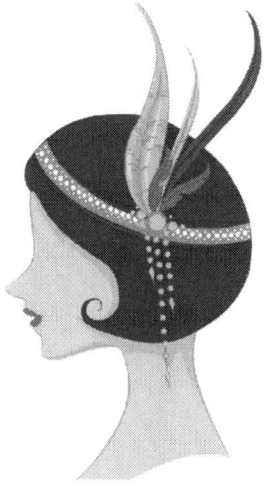

Acknowledgements

My critique partners, Laurie Snow Turner, Mary Malcarne Thomas and Lisa McKendrick
So many critique groups are overly critical. I have found with you guys a happy medium of encouragement, cheerleading and constructive suggestions. Thank you.
My proof-reader – Tami Stewart and Anna Lankford
The mothers of a large and growing families who read like the wind with an eagle eye. Thank you for finding little errors that have been missed.
My editor – Jolene Perry of Waypoint Author Academy
Sending my work to editors is the most terrifying part of the process for me but Jolene offers correction and constructive criticism without crushing my fragile ego.
My cheerleader, marketer and IT guy – Todd Matern
A lot of the time during the marketing side of being an author I am running around with my hair on fire. Todd is the yin to my yang. He calms me down and takes over when I am yelling at the computer.
My beta readers – Francesca Matern, Stina Van Cott,
Your reactions to my characters and plot are invaluable.
The Writing Gals for their FB author community and their YouTube tutorials
These ladies give so much of their time to teaching their Indie author followers how to succeed in this brave new publishing world. Thank you.

Printed in Great Britain
by Amazon